Modinama

Modinama

Issues That Did Not Matter

Subhash Gatade

LeftWord

First published in June 2019

LeftWord Books
2254/2A Shadi Khampur
New Ranjit Nagar
New Delhi 110008
INDIA

LeftWord Books is the publishing division of
Naya Rasta Publishers Pvt. Ltd.

leftword.com

ISBN 978-81-934666-9-8

Printed and bound by Chaman Enterprises, Delhi

For Ravi Sinha

CONTENTS

A hero of our time, gentlemen, is in fact a portrait, but not of an individual; it is the aggregate of the vices of our whole generation in their fullest expression.

Mikhail Lermontov, *A Hero of our Time*, 1840

PREFACE: *MODI 2*

> The crisis consists precisely in the fact that the old is dying and the new cannot be born; in this interregnum a great variety of morbid symptoms appear.
>
> – Antonio Gramsci, *Prison Notebooks*, 1930

Narendra Damodardas Modi, the man who began his political journey as a pracharak of the Rashtriya Swayamsevak Sangh (RSS), has been re-elected Prime Minister of India. This is the first time that a right-wing Hindutva government has been able to return to power. The last right-wing Hindutva government (1998-2004) was voted out of office. Modi's party – the Bharatiya Janata Party (BJP) – and his bloc – the National Democratic Alliance (NDA) – have garnered more seats and a higher vote share than they did in 2014. Amongst the parliamentarians of the BJP in the Lok Sabha there will be not one Muslim, the largest religious minority in India (with a population of over 200 million people).

Amartya Sen, the Nobel laureate, had said that India has taken a 'quantum jump in the wrong direction since 2014'. The very idea of India, Sen and others said, was at stake in this election. This was set aside, as almost one in two Indians who voted chose a party of the NDA. The enthusiasm, the vigour, the frenzy exhibited by the supporters of the BJP and the NDA is an indication that they are fascinated by the 'New India' of Modi, a new India with new icons that have little resemblance to the India that emerged out of the freedom movement.

PREFACE

The results of the Lok Sabha election of 2019 have shocked many, but the signs that pointed towards them had become clear. Modi and the BJP held tightly to the levers of power. Their commitment to the principles and values of the Indian Constitution is formal. They have no qualms about subverting the institutional checks and balances forged by the drafters of the Constitution. They are interested in recasting the Republic of India into a state that belongs to the majority religion, and to render invisible a numerically significant minority. They demonize the 'internal enemy', whether it be the religious minority or the political dissenter. They peddle a myth that India equals Hindu India – being no less than the vision of the RSS and its affiliates. Modi and the BJP have been able to create a broad constituency that cuts across the barriers of caste and region, promoted by state power and by the sprawling network of affiliated organizations of the Sangh Parivar. This constituency fuelled the re-election of Modi – more Modi than anything.

Is it enough to say that India is caught between its secular past and its communal future? This book, based on a look at the first five years of Modi's reign, goes beyond that dichotomy. Even in the secular past there were trends of social hierarchy and religious intolerance that Modi was able to elaborate upon. The idea of the 'external enemy' and the 'arch rival', the easy way in which jingoism could be mobilized around the Pulwama terror attack, the surrender of the war-mongering embedded media – all this shows the depth of the rot.

When the dust settles people will analyse how the elections were influenced by the rapid spread of social media – especially WhatsApp groups – and by the amount of money spent on the election. All this is true. But the media and money were only successful because they were able to inflame right-wing sentiments that had been cultivated by the Sangh Parivar over the past several decades. Voices of moderation and inclusion were silenced. Issues of life and livelihood – including the distress of farmers, unemployment, inflation – found no traction.

It is a time of deep introspection for the opposition – from the regional parties to the Left, as well as civil society organizations. All those who yearn for a plural and inclusive India have to think about why conversations of life and livelihood did not dominate the election; why the thuggery of the Hindutva vigilantes seems inconsequential to vast numbers of ordinary, decent people; why an aggressive, masculine fundamentalism is so normalized in our society today.

In other words, why didn't the issues that matter, seem to matter? Was it money and the media or was there a higher barrier? To some extent the answer can be found in the fragmentation of the opposition, with insufficient alliances built in key parts of the country. But the question we have raised goes deeper than electoral arithmetic. It asks if Modi and the BJP have not only changed the electoral map, but also begun to corrode social norms.

In his first speech after the 2019 election, Modi said he would uphold the Constitution. The five years of his first tenure have demonstrated quite visibly the great hiatus which has existed between what he claims and what he does. It would be the height of innocence to assume that the coming period will be any different. This book, based on a journey through Modi's first five years as prime minister, is a warning for the next five.

The author would like to especially thank Sudhanva Deshpande for agreeing to publish this book at such short notice. Special thanks are due to Vijay Prashad, for making the manuscript more readable.

PREFACE

This book is dedicated to long-time friend and comrade Ravi Sinha, leading Marxist scholar and activist, who is also the best teacher I have ever met.

INTRODUCTION: *IDEAS AS CRIMES*

> To such a degree has Religion fuelled conflict, complicated politics, retarded social development and impaired human relations across the world, that one is often tempted to propose that Religion is innately an enemy of Humanity, if not indeed of itself a crime against Humanity . . . it is time that the world adopted a position that refuses to countenance Religion as an acceptable justification for – excuse or extenuation of – crimes against Humanity.
>
> – Wole Soyinka, 'Religion Against Humanity', 2012

Words, ideas scare fundamentalists of every kind, every colour and every stripe.

The faithful are unwilling to question anything in their 'holy books'. If anything is challenged, it unnerves them. They react in the only way that they know: they resort to machetes to take on ideas and use meat cleavers to deal with unchained minds, hacking away at sensitive people as they take refuge in their 'books of wisdom'.

Modern critique of sacred books of any religion poses a serious dilemma to the followers of these books. It also poses a problem for those who believe in democracy.

What should one say if these sacred books have references to the burning of infidels on stakes, or if these books permit a man to marry many women, if they instruct rulers to cut a person's tongue or to pour hot lead into a person's ears if this person sings or listens to religious hymns? What to do if the interpreters of these books order its devotees to keep away from certain places of worship or if these interpreters harass women?

Should a critical intellectual look the other way, pretending that what is in plain sight is not seen? Should the intellectual rationalize such acts to reinforce faith or should the intellectual offer a mild rebuke that such acts do not match modern values?

What should a modern state – which claims to be secular – do in such cases? Should it facilitate the flourishing of such critiques? Or should it allow the fanatics of different shades to use violence against critics as a defence of their sacred books?

Our times – the explosion of religion into politics – is witness to the stigmatization of the criticism of religion. This stigmatization is not benign. It has led to planned murders and assassinations of writers, rationalists and cultural workers. It has led to the bombing of progressive cultural festivals. It has led to the attack on shrines that celebrate the compositeness of our culture.

South Asia has become the epicentre of such violence. The past decade has been especially sharp with regard to these killings and attacks.

Pakistan. Salman Taseer was the governor of Punjab (Pakistan). He supported a hapless Christian woman, Aasiya Noreen (known as Asia Bibi), who was languishing in prison under the charge of blasphemy. Taseer not only supported her but he called for the entire idea of blasphemy to be removed from Pakistan's statute books. On 4 January 2011, Salman Taseer was shot to death by his own bodyguard, Mumtaz Qadri. A few days before he was murdered, Taseer said that he would continue down the path against the blasphemy laws even if 'he is the last man standing'. A few months later, on 2 March 2011, Shahbaz Bhatti – the Federal Minister for Minority Affairs – was killed for similar reasons. Seven years later, Aasiya Noreen was freed and allowed to leave Pakistan. The blasphemy laws remain intact.

Bangladesh. On 15 February 2013, neo-fascist Islamists entered the home of Ahmad Rajib Haider, a young blogger. They assassinated him with their machetes. This was at a time when the Shahbagh movement was at its peak. People gathered at Dhaka's Shahbagh to demand that the criminals who backed Pakistani repression in the 1971 war – mostly associated with the Jamaat-e-Islami – be brought to justice. Haider was a strong critic of Islamic fundamentalism and of Islamist political groups. He used to write about them on his blog and on other social networking sites. Rajib Haider was part of a bloggers' group which spearheaded a direct confrontation with the neo-fascist Islamists. A month before Haider was assassinated, another member of his group – the blogger Asif Mohiuddin – was attacked outside his house by four youths from the Ansarullah Bangla Team that they had formed (inspired by the Yemeni cleric Anwar al-Awlaki). On 7 March 2013, another blogger and online activist Sunnyur Rahman (known as *Nastik Nobi* or Atheist Prophet) was stabbed. The killings did not cease. On 11 June 2018, Shahzahan Bachchu, the owner of *Bishaka Prokashoni* – a publishing house – was killed in his hometown of Munshiganj.

India. India, which claims to be the 'biggest democracy in the world', does not look any different from its neighbours when it comes to this kind of violence. The assassins have been as effective, but here the state has been less willing than in Pakistan and Bangladesh to pursue the cases to justice. The killers of Taseer and Rajib Haider have been caught and punished. No such alacrity is in evidence in India. Here are a list of the most well-known people to be killed within the past few years:

> Narendra Dabholkar, murdered on 20 August 2013 in his hometown of Pune (Maharashtra), was an anti-superstition activist. His murderers have not been found.

> Govind Pansare was murdered on 20 February 2015 as he returned home from his morning walk. He was a communist leader and the author of several important books on history and culture, including his study of Shivaji. He was killed in his hometown of Kolhapur (Maharashtra).
>
> M.M. Kalburgi was a scholar of Vachana Sahitya and a noted epigraphist. He was murdered on 30 August 2015 in the town of Dharwad (Karnataka), where he had spent his career at Karnataka University.
>
> Gauri Lankesh, editor of *Lankesh Patrike*, was an activist against communalism. She was gunned down at the door of her house on 5 September 2017.

These are the most well known of those killed. There are many others, such as A. Farooq (age 31), a scrap iron dealer who was a member of the Periyarist organization Dravidar Viduthalai Kazhagam. On 18 March 2017, he was killed on the streets of Coimbatore (Tamil Nadu) by a member of a neo-fascist Islamist organization for his outspoken atheistic and rationalist views that he posted on Facebook and on a WhatsApp group.

Targeted killings and assassinations are not the only way to silence dissenting voices. Many insidious ways are available for that. The most widely used method is to file a frivolous case against writers, novelists, cultural workers and activists. The accusation is often the same – that these people 'hurt religious sentiments'. Friends of Gauri Lankesh recall how the Hindutva fanatics had filed more than two dozen cases against her in different parts of Karnataka. They targeted her writings, wanting their pressure to muzzle her.

Gone are the days of openly expressing disagreement or of

a healthy public debate. The emphasis now is on criminalizing opinions that do not suit the dominant classes. If you are not ready to be a cheerleader or a passive observer, then you are not safe: that is the message from the ruling elites. If you are a professor who accepts the status quo, then you are safe. If you are a professor who dissents, then you are not safe. Trade unionists, activists, editors, journalists, professors – anybody can be charged with any crime and condemned to rot in India's jails for years thanks to the draconian laws that the government utilizes.

The criminalization of dissent is not new. But it has certainly become more forceful under the rule of the Hindutva fanatics at the Centre and in many states. A new aggression is evident. *The Hoot* – a website that monitors the media in the country and publishes regular reports – has provided a table to demonstrate the changes inside India's media landscape. The table below lists the cases filed against writers, media personalities and activists. What is evident is the quantum leap in cases filed under the headings of Sedition and Defamation. This leap took place within two years of the Hindutva fanatics taking power at the Centre. The data is a warning to dissenters.

	2014	2015	2016	
Sedition	0	0	11	(19 people)
Defamation	4	2	28	
Deaths	0	1	1	
Attacks	4	5	21	
Censorship	16	2	17	
Threats	5	1	7	

The trend of criminalization of dissent is also evident in the states. In Assam, the government reported that 'as many as 245 sedition cases were registered across 17 districts since the Bharatiya Janata Party-led alliance came to power in the state in 2016'.

On closer scrutiny one discovers that an unholy alliance of sorts seems to have emerged between the corporate czars, custodians of state power and dominant religious/ethnic communities which has resulted in crushing the voices of reason and of dissent. People who are under the impression that such cases do not have any impact on journalists, writers, intellectuals are sadly mistaken. Journalists who had been sued by a leading corporate house (the Ambanis) told Vijayta Lalwani of *Scroll* (29 December 2018) that they have been shrouded with a veil of silence. Intimidation sets the tone.

Things have reached such a maddening proportion that even the Supreme Court was forced to sound a warning bell when a case was filed against Mahendra Singh Dhoni, the well-known cricketer for 'hurting religious sentiments' when he was depicted as Lord Vishnu on a magazine cover. Rejecting the petition filed against Dhoni, a bench made up of Justices Dipak Misra, A.M. Khanwilkar and M.M. Shantanagoudar said that 'insults to religion offered unwittingly or carelessly or without any deliberate or malicious intention to outrage the religious feelings of that class' should not be seen as hurting religious sentiments.

An RSS leader – Suresh Bhaiyyaji Joshi – accused the Indian Supreme Court in 2018 of hurting the 'sentiments of Hindus' when it deferred taking up the Ayodhya title dispute case – to adjudicate the issue of the Babri Masjid and its land. The Court said it had 'more important issues' to take up, to which Joshi said that the Court had hurt the sentiments of 'crores of Hindus'. One heard similar complaints when the Supreme Court intervened in the Sabarimala issue, ordering the temple to allow women in their 'menstruating years' to be allowed into the Sabarimala complex. Leader after leader of the RSS and the BJP – and many Congress leaders as well – questioned this judgment and called for subordination of the law to a hierarchical idea of tradition.

Hurt has become a common standard.

In Kerala, Muslim organizations protested when a girl delivered the *azaan* (call to prayer) in a play in Kozhikode. The play – *Kithab* – tells the story of a girl's dream to call out the *azaan* like her father – a maulvi. The Muslim Students Federation and the Social Democratic Party of India denounced this as an 'insult to the Muslim way of life' and said that only men can call the *azaan*. *Kithab* raises the precise question of what a Muslim girl can and cannot do. When the girl wants to act in a play, the father locks her up to prevent her performance. The play, which had been a great success, is now sidelined.

The argument of 'hurt sentiments' is simple: if an individual or even the Supreme Court dares to disagree with the interpretation of reality offered by the neo-fascists, then they will have to face the consequences. These are often very violent.

Books are often junked for being accused of 'hurting sentiments'. A.K. Ramanujan's seminal essay, 'Three Hundred Ramayanas', was removed from the syllabus of Delhi University. Wendy Doniger's book, *The Hindus: An Alternative History*, was dumped when the neo-fascists threatened violence. These works were removed when the BJP was not in power. When the BJP came to power at the Centre in 2014, the party's ascent emboldened its cadre to use state patronage and street power against dissenters. Even texts that communicate the personal experience of the writer are forbidden – Om Prakash Valmiki's *Joothan*, Perumal Murugan's work, Sowvendra Hansda Shekhar's writings and Kancha Iliah's *Why I am not a Hindu*. People are told how to comprehend their own life experiences.

Ideas are crimes. In George Orwell's *1984* (1948), he provides us with the concept of illegal thoughts – Thought crimes. If you hold unspoken beliefs or doubts that oppose the ruling elites, then these are considered thought crimes. They do not even have to be articulated. The government attempts to control not only the speech of people or their writings, but also their thoughts. We are creeping in that direction, not only in India but in large parts of South Asia. We are creeping into dystopia.

ONE. *UNDER THE SHADOW OF THE HOLY BOOK*

> Not everything that is faced can be changed, but nothing can be changed until it is faced.
>
> – James Baldwin, 1962

Democracy is in trouble. Populists and demagogues have emerged to power. The Strongmen – Trump, Putin, Erdogan, Duterte – are an indicator of the problem. They are stoking a fascination with illiberal ideologies amongst large numbers of people. The concern for democracy's future is not misplaced.

The arrival of Narendra Damodardas Modi – the Prime Minister of India – must be looked at in this context. Modi began his political life as a *pracharak* of the RSS, an exclusivist organization of Hindu men. Modi paid his respects before parliament on his first visit there with the famous declaration that Parliament is the 'temple of democracy' and that the Constitution is the 'most sacred book to him'. Modi repeated this gesture on many occasions – in his address in the Lok Sabha as part of the commemoration of the Constitution to mark the 125th birth anniversary of the chairman of its drafting committee, Dr. B.R. Ambedkar, and then again in his address to a joint meeting of the US Congress in Washington, D.C. The Constitution, he said, is a holy book.

But the Constitution is not a holy book. It is not – as the dictionary puts it – a 'divinely inspired statement of . . . faith, history and practices'. It is drafted by people and should be seen as such.

A section of liberals heard Modi's sentiment and felt a sense of hope. They saw this as a signal that Modi now intends to break from his controversial past and would like to forge a new beginning. This was seen as somehow a departure from the controversial relationship of the RSS to the Indian Constitution. It is now history how the RSS wanted the Indian Constitution of 1950 be withdrawn in favour of the *Manusmriti* (dated to be from the 2nd to the 3rd century BCE) and how its fascination towards it still continues unabated.

Would Modi uphold, defend and strengthen the Constitution, and thereby ensure – as Dr. Ambedkar had said – that India move from a political democracy (one individual, one vote) to a social democracy (with the citizenry enriched by each other)? This was not Modi's road. His road was *jumla* (empty promise). Perhaps Modi's was not an empty promise. Perhaps Modi had in mind the holy books of the ancient world, the books known to defend the status quo based on inequity and exclusion, books that ask their adherents to adopt hierarchy and obediently discharge their duties ordained to them at birth and await their reward in the afterlife.

When Modi, newly elected, went to reply to the motion of thanks to the President's address to the joint session of parliament, he said something of great significance. He said, '*Barah sau saal ki gulami ki maansikta humein pareshan kar rahi hai. Bahut baar humse thoda ooncha vyakti mile, to sar ooncha karke baat karne ki humari taaqat nahin hoti hai* (The slave mentality of 1,200 years is troubling us. Often, when we meet a person of high stature, we fail to muster the strength to speak up).' The key phrase here is 'slave mentality of 1,200 years'. Modi offered a new interpretation of Indian history. His was a paradigm shift from what we had learned in school. We had learned of the 'slavery of 200 years' – the years of colonial rule. Now, Modi increased the time period to the 'slave mentality of 1,200 years'. What Modi did here was to erase the difference between the era of colonialism – under the British Raj – and the earlier kingdoms, many of them ruled by Muslim rulers. This is the RSS view that the 'Muslims' are alien to India, that 'they' have ruled 'us' for a thousand years.

I

A Constitution is an imperfect document, a document that is at the heart of a democracy with the citizenry guided by it and able to change it to keep it dynamic. A holy book – a sacred book – claims to be superior to the people and to be infallible. There is no way to reasonably compare a democratic Constitution to a holy book.

Holy books take hundreds of years for even minor changes. It took 359 years for the Roman Catholic Church to change its stand regarding Galileo Galilei. At an inquisition held in 1633, the Church had forced Galileo to recant his views that the earth moves around the sun. Only in 1992 did the Church declare that Galileo was right. On the other hand, our Constitution has been amended over a hundred times in the past 68 years.

The spirit of the Constitution is not akin to the spirit of most holy books. The Constitution of India's Preamble opens with great promise. The words are in capitals: JUSTICE, LIBERTY, EQUALITY and FRATERNITY. They are emphasized. These are not words from ancient texts. It would be anachronistic to search for them there. They required the anti-colonial mass movement to bring them to the front of the Constitution, which is itself the fruit of that mass struggle against colonialism and imperialism. It is worth quoting the Preamble in full:

> We, the people of India, having solemnly resolved to constitute

India into a SOVEREIGN, SOCIALIST, SECULAR, DEMOCRATIC REPUBLIC and to secure to all its citizens:

JUSTICE, social, economic and political;

LIBERTY of thought, expression, belief, faith and worship;

EQUALITY of status and of opportunity;

and to promote among them all FRATERNITY assuring the dignity of the individual and the unity and integrity of the Nation ... ENACT AND GIVE TO OURSELVES THIS CONSTITUTION.

The test of the Constitution is whether a government is able to advance the cause of these principles, to deepen democracy to the underprivileged, the marginalized and the disadvantaged – especially to the Dalits and the Adivasis and to the other marginalized populations.

II

Almost seventy years ago, the Indian Constitution came into effect with its solemn declaration about the abolition of discrimination on the basis of caste, religion, sex and ethnicity. The words of the Constitution are vivid.

But there are warning signs. In the 16th Lok Sabha, the ruling party – the BJP – did not have one single Muslim member. The percentage of Muslims in parliament was the lowest since the '60s. The BJP nominated very few Muslims, and since the BJP won a majority the absence of Muslims is directly linked to the BJP's nomination decisions. It was not inadvertent. It appears to have been deliberate.

The gradual marginalization of Muslims – and other religious minorities – is a symptom of a great churning in society, where Muslims – and others – are beginning to feel redundant because of the policies of the government. They are increasingly being told to adopt an 'Indian' (namely Hindu) way of life and they are often told that their places of worship (mosques) are not integral to their religious identity.

Satish Deshpande, who teaches sociology at the University of Delhi, wrote in 2015 that there are attempts on to 'cultivate a far more durable system of normalized oppression' in which Muslims are 'compelled to become permanent participants in their own subordination'. 'The key element here,' he writes, 'would be the imposition of conditionalities limiting the extent and quality of their citizenship. Once the basic principle of subordinate citizenship is legitimized, all the old cliches extolling happy coexistence, syncretic culture, the inherent tolerance of Hinduism, etc., could be brazenly repeated – *garv se*.'

Democracy is built on shared ideals and goals rather than on shared hatreds and exclusions.

Old discriminations have not been eradicated in modern India.

Manual scavenging is banned in India and has been banned not once but twice (in 1993 and then in 2013). But the situation on the ground is unchanged. About eight lakh people are engaged in this profession, 95 per cent of them women.

Dowry is banned in India. The Dowry Prohibition Act of 1961 and two sections of the Indian Penal Code make it abundantly clear that dowry is illegal. Yet, there are eight thousand dowry deaths in India – a woman killed each hour for a practice that has been illegal for decades.

New bands of ruffians – lynch mobs and vigilante groups – are on the roads looking to capture those whom they consider to be worthy of violence. Protection of the cow comes before protection of humans. Communal incidents, all against the law, are not prosecuted. As vigilante violence increases, the state stands mute – either in connivance with the perpetrators or else standing at a distance from the violence. Trust in the rule of law suffers as the underprivileged find themselves more and more vulnerable to extreme violence.

India is slowly metamorphosing into a most unequal society, with the 1 per cent – the super-rich – getting richer, with half of the country's total wealth in their bank accounts (many offshore). The policies adopted by the ruling elite benefit the rich and are detrimental to the poor.

These vectors – violence and money – continue to undermine the Constitution.

III

What is democracy? It is a form of government in which all citizens participate equally. This participation either takes place through elected representatives or by direct action. Ideas of equality and liberty shape the institutions of a democracy. But a democracy would be empty if people were not active participants in fighting to improve their institutions and their society.

In our time, however, democracy is not experienced in this way. Ordinary people experience 'democracy' through the coercive machinery of the state – the police, the revenue department, and other authorities that seem to want something from them or that want to tell them how to behave.

One of the key ways in which a citizen understands or *feels* democracy is through the idea of the franchise. This idea comes in two directions: it implies the right to contest elections and it implies the right to choose one's representative without fear. India can rightly claim to be a democracy where the right to vote was granted to every adult – without any restrictions – at the time of Independence. In fact, it could be said that the anti-colonial struggle was a struggle for a universal adult franchise. The officials of the new India began preparations for the first draft electoral roll on the basis of universal adult franchise within a few months of independence, namely in November 1947. The delivery of a system based on universal adult franchise was the fulfilment of a commitment made during the national movement since the Nehru Report of 1928.

Indians imagined universal adult franchise for themselves, acting on this idea to craft a political reality. It is a different matter that with the passage of time, the attempt by the people to create a robust democracy has been squandered. The ruling elites have driven a policy to restrict democracy in subtle and not so subtle ways. The very idea of citizenship is now under threat. Proof is needed to show that one is a citizen. If one 'belongs' to an 'other' religion, then one is threatened with disenfranchisement. If you cannot fulfil the various tests, then you are struck from the electoral rolls. Twenty-one million women are not on the rolls in India. Seventeen million Dalits have been struck from the rolls in Maharashtra. These are the stories that are known. Others are off the rolls without fanfare.

In 2018, Bappa Sinha reported in *NewsClick* of a controversial programme – the National Electoral Roll Purification and Authentication Programme – that was put in place in 2015 to link the Aadhaar card to voter identification cards. The Supreme Court intervened to toss out the programme. The Chief Election Commissioner said that many people suspected that this programme would result in 'a number of deletions of names of voters from the electoral rolls'. In Telangana, two million people were removed from the rolls. 'In the process' of connecting Aadhaar to the voting rolls, Bappa Sinha writes, 'the data of millions of citizens was shared in a manner that violated their fundamental right to privacy'.

The situation in Assam – and in the North-East in general – is more troubling. In late 2018, the United Nations raised concerns about the question of the 'statelessness' of millions of Muslims in Assam. The government had struck their names from the National Register of Citizens (NRC). In a letter to the External Affairs Minister Sushma Swaraj, four UN Special Rapporteurs wrote,

> It is alleged that the Tribunals have been declaring large numbers of Bengali Muslims in Assam as foreigners, resulting in statelessness and risk of detention. Finally, it is alleged that the potential discriminatory effects of the updated NRC should be seen in light of the history of discrimination and violence faced by Muslims of Bengali origin due to their status as ethnic, religious and linguistic minority and their perceived foreignness. Although the Bengali origin Muslims in Assam descend from peasant workers brought from the former Bengal and East Bengal starting in the 19th century under colonial rule, they have long been portrayed as irregular migrants. As a result of this rhetoric, Bengali Muslims have historically been the target of various human rights violations, including forced displacement, arbitrary expulsions and killings.

These words should shock any sensitive person.

In the midst of the fiasco in Assam, the Joint Parliamentary Committee began to consider an amendment to the Citizenship Act of 1955. In the garb of humanitarianism, the amendment proposed to introduce the idea of a *right to return*, namely the right of certain people (Hindus) to be welcomed into India while others are not welcomed. This is the kind of narrow (racist) policy that is used by Israel. The Delhi Action Committee for Assam noted in 2016,

> The proposed amendment is premised on the religious persecution of non-Muslim minorities in neighbouring Muslim majority countries.

While religious basis has 'softly' underlined India's approaches to the issue of immigration since the Partition, what is alarming with the amendment proposed by the current government is its vehement attempt, in the garb of humanitarianism, to upturn the Constitution of India by slyly trying to introduce religious right-to-return. The current government displays zero or very little humanitarian concern for non-Hindu marginalized communities in the country and in neighbouring countries.

IV

The idea of citizenship is under threat. This has a direct bearing on democracy in action. This is one problem. Another is that the government has been raising barriers of various kinds to deprive people of the experience of contesting elections. Local government – the Panchayati Raj institutions, for example – are the first to face these barriers. Barriers include how many children the candidate has and whether the candidate has a home. If you have too many children or have no toilet – both more common amongst the working class – then you cannot run for elections.

In two BJP-ruled states, the government has added in an education requirement as a criterion for being a candidate in an election. This is unheard of in India. After the BJP lost the election in Rajasthan in 2018, the rules were rescinded by the Congress government. In Haryana, however, you now need a minimum educational qualification to contest elections. By the new standard, 70 to 84 per cent of the population has been deemed unfit. Most of those who will not be allowed to be candidates are from backward caste and Scheduled Caste communities. The judiciary has ratified this 'externment' of the people from democracy.

We are gradually moving – by this logic – towards a *managed* or *guided democracy*, a democracy with the elites in charge.

Why are so many people in these states deprived of education, and so deprived of democracy? Is this their fault? The onus has to be on the state, which has made insufficient arrangements to educate the population. People are being penalized for the inadequacy of the state. Despite a decade of the Right of Children to Education Act (2009), there has been hardly any movement towards universal education in India. A look at the situation as it exists today despite the decade old Right of Children to Free and Compulsory Education Act can prove an eye-opener in this regard.

A PIL filed by the Akhil Delhi Prathmik Shikshak Sangh before the Supreme Court had stated how children suffer as government schools shut down and as the government leaves 9.5 lakh posts for teachers vacant. A stunning 3.68 crore children are not in school. This is shocking. This data, says the Akhil Delhi Prathmik Shikshak Sangh, shows 'systematic and widespread violations of children's rights to education across the country'. The writ was dismissed. Chief Justice Ranjan Gogoi said, 'Don't expect miracles. India is a huge, huge country. Priorities are many and certainly, education is one of the priorities.' But not one to focus on apparently.

Education as a barrier is powerful. Since there is so little motivation to fulfil the priorities of the Right of Children to Free and Compulsory Education Act, it is likely that the barriers will be hard to surmount for millions of people for years to come. Local self-government institutions will remain in the control of the dominant castes and the ruling class. Such barriers could just as easily make their way towards the state Assemblies and to the Lok Sabha.

Barriers of education are not the only method to silence a section of the population. Consensus, which appears to be a benign idea, has been used effectively to disenfranchise large parts of the population. The villages of Ralegan Siddhi and Hiware

Bazaar (both in Maharashtra) are often used as examples for consensus governance. But here the ex-military man Anna Hazare (in Ralegan Siddhi) and Popatrao Pawar (in Hiware Bazaar) drove the agenda in the name of 'consensus'.

A study by the economics department at Mumbai University, published in *Economic & Political Weekly* in 2015 ('Culture, Community and Institutions: Voluntary Provision of Public Goods in Maharashtra') by Neeraj Hatekar, Parinaaz Mehta and Savita Kulkarni, found that consensus did not shape the projects. 'The findings suggest that the norm of cooperation and collective action is more fragile,' they write. 'Their stability depends crucially on monitoring and punishment mechanisms. It, therefore, appears that the established history of norms may not always inculcate the stable preference of "unconditional cooperation" in an individual's value system.' What they found was silence of the people, whose silence was taken as consensus. The silence was most pronounced amongst women and oppressed castes.

Ralegan Siddhi and Hiware Bazaar are not exceptions. In the early 1990s, the government introduced a *Samaras Gram Panchayat* scheme, which called for 'governance through consensus'. This scheme asked people to vote unanimously for an entire panchayat leadership, with an incentive being that they would then get additional funds for development. This project has now morphed, under the BJP, into a mechanism to reproduce dominant-caste power. The BJP sees these consensus panchayat mechanisms to be a 'unique custom of Arya culture'. This concept of 'Arya culture' was adopted by the state of Gujarat for its *Samras-yojana* scheme. Here elections are effectively annulled in the service of protecting the 'originality, events, customs' of the village. This 'unique Arya culture' is nothing other than the *varna*-based caste system, with the dominant castes in power. Apart from the handing over of the reins of the village panchayats to the dominant castes in the locality via the idea of consensus, we are also witness to the multiple ways in which the corporates now exercise power through local village governance.

In 2015, in a Congress-dominated area of Ernakulam district, a corporate house – Anna-Kitex – won the Kizhakkambalam Gram Panchayat elections. It had put up a slate, which swept the elections. The outgoing president of the panchayat – Jolly Baby – told the press that the elected officials had denied Anna-Kitex licences because they feared the contamination of water and wetlands by industrial development. 'It's a corporate takeover of the panchayat,' said P. Rajeev of the Communist Party of India (Marxist). The elected representatives are salaried employees of a private corporation.

Consensus suffocates democracy; corporates masquerade as democracy. And then, in 'conflict zones', the full machinery of the state is used to throttle the rights of the panchayats if they seem ready to resist the takeover of their lands by the corporate houses. Democracy becomes a shell. Voices are silenced. Democratic institutions are taken over by business and by fanatics. In Chhattisgarh, not only has the state suppressed panchayats on grounds of the anti-Maoist campaign, but Hindu-majority panchayats have passed resolutions to prevent Christian villagers from building churches.

There are now 2.5 lakh panchayats with 32 lakh panchayat representatives (including 12 lakh women). This is a considerable achievement. But beneath and around them, a hollowing out of the entire panchayati raj experiment is ongoing. This is a tragedy.

V

The experience of democracy is nothing if economic rights are not central to the lives of the citizenry. The BJP government came to power with the slogan *Sabka Saath, Sabka Vikas* (With Everyone, For Everyone's Development). It had before it instruments and laws set in place by previous governments, not all of them implemented effectively enough.

In 2005, the parliament passed the Right to Information Act. It helped to widen the question of accountability and transparency. Five years later, parliament passed the Right of Children to Free and Compulsory Education Act. In 2013, the parliament passed the Food Security Act. As a stop gap measure to tackle the hunger crisis, the government in 2005 passed the National Rural Employment Guarantee Act. It is important to point out that these acts came when the United Progressive Alliance -- with outside support from the Communists – was in power. These acts of parliament increased the possibility for people to improve their economic rights. These initiatives proved most beneficial to the most marginalized in society – namely Dalits and Adivasis. The Right to Information Act allowed people to demand information from the government machinery, while the National Rural Employment Guarantee Act provided work during days of scarcity.

No deep research is needed to understand how these rights have – since the BJP came to power – been scuttled. The BJP used legal fiat to do its job, as well as deprivation of funds to hire officials to fulfil the mandate of these acts. Funds dried up, institutions closed down and leadership was provided to the institutions of social welfare to undermine them.

The BJP cut down the National Rural Employment Guarantee Act, saying that it was a 'symbol of failure of the Congress government'. It allotted a few thousand crores, but it tried to hide the fact that a fourth of the amount allotted was for payments owed in previous years. The BJP did not implement the Food Security Act till 2016, and even then extended the deadline with executive orders. India ranks 103rd among 119 countries in the Global

Hunger Index. It sits below Bangladesh and Ethiopia. Education was not to be on the agenda of the BJP. Rajasthan – which had put educational requirements for candidates of the panchayat – closed down thousands of schools in the name of rationalization. The Rajasthani policy has now been followed across India. Maharashtra has now shut down 4,000 government schools with the claim that they had ten or fewer students. Private companies are now to open schools in the state. It is clear that as government schools close, the poor – mainly Dalits and Adivasis – will be without a place to study.

VI

There can be no democracy if individual rights are not defended and if the socio-cultural rights of people are not facilitated. Dr. Ambedkar described the 'constitutional morality' that is needed to transcend 'social morality'. The norms of society need to be brought into coherence with the norms of the Constitution.

Individual rights, the choices of people, are under attack by the state and by right-wing vigilante groups. The right to wear what one wants, the right to marry whom one wants and the right to eat what kind of food one would like is constrained by state action and by right-wing militia attacks.

A major eight-year study by the Anthropological Survey of India (AnSI), completed in 1993, went over every custom and habit of every single community in India. Directed by Kumar Suresh Singh, the AnSI study found that of the 4,635 communities in India a good 88 per cent are meat-eaters. A 2006 *State of the Nation* survey conducted by the Centre for the Study of Developing Societies reinforced the AnSI study. It found that the overwhelming majority of the people in India are non-vegetarians, and that at most 31 per cent of the population are vegetarians. The real divide in India is not between vegetarians and non-vegetarians, but between the hungry and the non-hungry.

Hunger is a central part of the Indian experience. Rather than find a way to feed people, the BJP and its vigilante groups are seized on what one should or should not eat. It is a cruel attitude to hunger.

In Gujarat, the government bowed to the demands of a section of the Jain community who wanted Palitana (near Bhavnagar), a sacred place for Jains, turned into a 'vegetarian area'. This was done just as Modi became prime minister. Ritual slaughter of animals was banned in the zone, and an estimated 260 butcher shops were closed. Restaurants that sold meat closed down. This was a premonition of things to come.

Eating food became criminalized. With the banning of beef, Dalits and Muslims have faced violent attacks. The ban has directly impacted the livelihood of people who have been made redundant, and it has created mayhem on fields as stray cattle are now eating the crops. Meanwhile, the vast majority of people – Dalits, Adivasis, Muslims, Christians – are deprived of a cheap source of protein, namely beef. Beef costs one third the price of mutton. It forms an important part of the traditional food of many people. Their traditions are irrelevant. Only the traditions of the powerful castes are important.

Beef is not the only meat to face sanctions. Other non-vegetarian foods came under scrutiny. 'Illegal abattoirs' were closed down and distribution of eggs – in some places – was stopped for the midday meal schemes. Basic delivery of protein was hampered.

The party – BJP – that opposes beef consumption in general has no qualms in claiming that in other states where it hopes to make electoral gains (Kerala and Goa as well as in the North-East) it promises good quality beef and says that beef eating is no impediment to be a member of the RSS.

Not only did the government disregard the problem of hunger, it also disregarded complaints about caste discrimination. The government sent a weak representative to the courts to defend the Prevention of Atrocities Act, and then did not complain when the two judges of the Supreme Court bench diluted the legislation. The government took months to issue an ordinance, despite the fact that government records show that atrocities against Dalits and Adivasis have increased. Only later was the BJP government compelled to justify the decision to amend the Prevention of Atrocities Act 'to overturn the Supreme Court verdict to introduce anticipatory bail provision, saying that people from the Scheduled Castes/Scheduled Tribes communities continue to face atrocities and they need protection'.

VII

How should people describe themselves? In a democracy, that is a fundamental right, the right to describe oneself, to affirm one's right to exist. This is a right closely held by oppressed communities, in India by Dalits and Adivasis. On 7 August 2018, the Ministry of Information and Broadcasting issued a circular that advised the media to refrain from using the word *Dalit* while referring to those belonging to Scheduled Castes. It said that the Constitutional term Scheduled Castes must be used in English and its translation in other national languages should alone be used for all official transactions. The Press Council of India said that such a ban was 'neither feasible nor advisable'.

The decision goes against the fundamental rights of equality (Article 14), non-discrimination (Article 15) and the right to life and liberty (Article 21) guaranteed under the Constitution. Sriram Parakkat, an advocate who represented various Dalit groups, challenged the Centre's circular before the Supreme Court. The plea by Parakkat said that the term *Dalit* is self-chosen, a 'positive self-identifier and a political identity'. The Court rejected the plea.

The majoritarian understanding of democracy, as driven by the BJP, has no space for such self-expression. The entire process reminds one of what Jayant Lele wrote in 1995 (*Hindutva: the Emergence of the Right*) of the three essential characteristics of Hindutva – 'hegemonic, homogenizing and pedagogic, all at the same time and in complex interrelated ways'. Hindutva seeks to dominate, it seeks to flatten and it seeks to convince even the oppressed of its worldview.

The question is not only how one describes oneself, but also how one perceives one's life experiences. Any reflection on the religion to which one is supposed to belong and the way that religion treats one is to be refracted through the ideology of Hindutva. That is why the BJP has targeted individual voices that offer a radically critical view of life under the caste system and of Hinduism – books such as Om Prakash Valmiki's *Joothan*, Perumal Murugan's writings and Sowvendra Hansda Shekhar's writings. This is why Kancha Iliah's *Why I am not a Hindu* is a threat. This is why they cannot be allowed in school or university curriculums.

Even Dr. Ambedkar cannot be himself. A sanitized and fictitious Dr. Ambedkar is presented, one who is close to Hindutva ideology, a 'Hindu Social Reformer' rather than a critic of Hinduism itself. The Maharashtra government demolished Ambedkar Bhavan, which was built by Dr. Ambedkar himself, to make way for a 17-floor commercial building. The demolition took place early on a Saturday morning. Office furniture, a printing press and a rare collection of books sunk into the earth. Books that did not get buried were destroyed by water.

Dr. Ambedkar cannot be allowed to be himself. The Gujarat government of the BJP commissioned a biography of Dr. Ambedkar for government schools. The author included Dr. Ambedkar's 22 pledges that his followers took when they converted to Buddhism in 1956. He had insisted upon a complete severance from Hinduism. The vows struck a blow at the root of Hindu beliefs and practices. The pledges are as follows:

1. I shall have no faith in Brahma, Vishnu and Mahesh nor shall I worship them.
2. I shall have no faith in Rama and Krishna who are believed to be incarnation of God nor shall I worship them.
3. I shall have no faith in 'Gauri', 'Ganapati' and other gods and goddesses of Hindus nor shall I worship them.
4. I do not believe in the incarnation of God.
5. I do not and shall not believe that Lord Buddha was the incarnation of Vishnu. I believe this to be sheer madness and false propaganda.
6. I shall not perform 'Shraddha' nor shall I give 'pind-dan'.
7. I shall not act in a manner violating the principles and teachings of the Buddha.
8. I shall not allow any ceremonies to be performed by Brahmins.
9. I shall believe in the equality of man.
10. I shall endeavour to establish equality.
11. I shall follow the 'noble eightfold path' of the Buddha.
12. I shall follow the 'paramitas' prescribed by the Buddha.
13. I shall have compassion and loving kindness for all living beings and protect them.
14. I shall not steal.
15. I shall not tell lies.
16. I shall not commit carnal sins.
17. I shall not take intoxicants like liquor, drugs etc.
18. I shall endeavour to follow the noble eightfold path and practise compassion and loving kindness in every day life.
19. I renounce Hinduism which is harmful for humanity and

impedes the advancement and development of humanity because it is based on inequality, and adopt Buddhism as my religion.

20. I firmly believe the Dhamma of the Buddha is the only true religion.
21. I believe that I am having a re-birth.
22. I solemnly declare and affirm that I shall hereafter lead my life according to the principles and teachings of the Buddha and his Dhamma.

As is clear, the vows asked the new Buddhists to liberate themselves from superstitions, wasteful and meaningless rituals. These had only increased the pauperization of the masses and the enrichment of the dominant castes. The vows asked the new Buddhists to have no faith in any Hindu god and to no longer worship them.

The government of Anandiben Patel, a close ally of Modi, destroyed lakhs of copies of the biography because of the presence of these vows.

VIII

The government's desire to define the identity of Dalits is not restricted to them alone. Much the same kind of formulations are used to confine Adivasis and other oppressed communities. The very word 'Adivasi' is in question. This means 'original inhabitant'. Hindutva ideology prefers the term Vanvasi – 'forest dweller'.

Adivasis cannot be seen to be prior to Hindus, to have any title to the soil that is above and beyond that demanded by the dominant castes. They have to be relegated to the forest. Adivasis are being slowly drawn into the net of Hindutva ideology. Hanuman statues are being erected in their localities, and new festivals such as Shabari Kumbh are being introduced to draw them into the affiliations of Hinduism and Hindutva. Programmes around *ghar wapsi* are in full swing – as Adivasis are being Hinduized. The Vanvasi communities are being pitted against their brethren who have adopted Christianity.

Goldy George, activist and social scientist, writes in a stimulating piece – 'Adivasis in Fascist Regime' – that there is a rushed 'sweeping pattern of Hinduization of learning and education spaces'. 'All Adivasi and Dalit hostels are used for this purpose. Saraswati Pooja has been one of the initial entries which in fact moved to other regimes of life with a critical substitution of many of the Adivasi and Dalit gods and goddesses.' A few years ago, a Hindu dominated panchayat in Chhattisgarh denied Christians the right to build a church. This is a panchayat led by the newly Hindutva-ized communities. Democracy was used to curtail basic rights. Attacks by Hindutva fanatics – amongst whom are many Adivasis – with the connivance of the police against Christians is routine.

There is no end in sight to this kind of madness, this suffocation of democracy, this life under the shadow of the holy book.

TWO. *LYNCHISTAN*

Seven decades have elapsed since India's first Prime Minister Jawaharlal Nehru said that the country had woken 'to life and freedom'. The long 'period of ill fortune' had ended and a new era had begun. Nowadays, Nehru's *Tryst with Destiny* speech is seen as passé. The women and men who fought to bring about that day – the independence of India – are now set aside, the memory of their struggle obliterated. Gone is the resolve to 'bring freedom and opportunity to the common man, to the peasants and workers of India; to fight and end poverty and ignorance and disease' and 'build up a prosperous, democratic and progressive nation'.

Ours is a New India, with a government that seeks to consciously dismantle all those social, economic and political institutions whose foundations were laid down to 'ensure justice and fullness of life to every man and woman', where the country's resolve not to encourage communalism or narrow-mindedness because 'no nation can be great whose people are narrow in thought or in action' is being watered down bit by bit. These words of Nehru were printed in *The Hindu* on 15 August 1947. They were a message to the people who had woken up to an independent India. But, the New India, the India of the current ruling class – whose instrument has been the BJP – is truly a different India, an India where debates are not encouraged, where differences are frowned upon and where dissent is criminalized. This is an India where mob rule has overwhelmed the rule of law, where cartoonists are arrested for mocking leaders under the charge of sedition. This last is a point to emphasize. Jawaharlal Nehru wrote to the leading cartoonist of his day – K. Shankar Pillai – to say, 'Don't spare me, Shankar.' He didn't.

Today, it is difficult to find many people who have fond memories of that historic speech or who feel a closeness to the great women and men who sacrificed their future for a better present. Who could imagine that one fine morning India would suddenly start to mirror its 'arch rival' – namely Pakistan – thereby vindicating Nehru's worst fears of India becoming a 'Hindu Pakistan'?

A few years ago, the leading progressive poet of Pakistan, Fahmida Riaz, captured the tensions in India in a beautiful poem. In her visit to India, Riaz suggested that she discovered a country no different from Pakistan. It was no coincidence that she read out her poem in India when the first BJP government was in power at the Centre. The poem is called *Tum bilkul hum jaise nikle*, or 'You turned out to be just like us'. It was written in 1996, with reference to the rise of communal violence in India – notably to the RSS-BJP driven riots after the destruction of the Babri Masjid in Ayodhya.

Tum bilkul hum jaisey nikley
Ab tak kahan chhupe the bhai
Voh moorkhta, voh ghaamarpan
Jis mein hum ne sadi ganwai
Aakhir pahunchi dwaar tumhaarey
Arre badhai bohot badhai
So it turned out you were just like us!
Where were you hiding all this time, buddy?
That stupidity, that ignorance
we wallowed in for a century –

look, it arrived at your shores too!
Many congratulations to you!

Preyt dharam ka naach rahaa hai
Qayam Hindu raaj karogey?
Saarey ultey kaaj karogey
Apna chaman daraaj karogey
Tum bhee baithey karogey sochaa
Poori hai waisi tayyari
Kaun hai Hindu, kaun naheen hai
Tum bhi karogey fatwe jaari
Hoga kathin yahan bhi jeena
Raaton aa jayega paseena
Jaisi taisi kata karegi
Yahan bhi sabki saans ghutegi
Kal dukh se socha karti thi
Soch ke bohot hansi aaj aee,
Tum bilkul hum jaise nikley
Hum do qaum nahin the bhai!
Raising the flag of religion,
I guess now you'll be setting up Hindu Raj?
You too will commence to muddle everything up
You, too, will ravage your beautiful garden.
You, too, will sit and ponder –
I can tell preparations are afoot –
who is [truly] Hindu, who is not.
I guess you'll be passing fatwas soon!
Here, too, it will become hard to survive.
Here, too, you will sweat and bleed.
You'll barely make do joylessly.
You will gasp for air like us.

I used to wonder with such deep sorrow.
And now, I laugh at the idea:
it turned out you were just like us!
We weren't two nations after all!

Bhaar mein jaaye shiksha viksha
Ab jaahilpan ke gun gaana.
Aage gaddha hai yeh mat dekho
Wapas laao gaya zamana
Bhasht karo tum aajayega
Ulte paaon chalte jaana
Dhyaan na mann mein dooja aaye
Bas peechhe hi nazar jamana
Ek jaap saa kartey jao
Baaram baar yahi dohrao
Kitna veer mahaan tha Bharat
Kaisa alishaan tha Bharat
Phir tum log pohonch jaogay
Bas parlok pohonch jaogay
Hum toh hain pehle se wahan par
Tum bhi samay nikalte rehna
Ab jis nark mein jaao wahan se
Chitthi vitthi daalte rehna
To hell with education and learning.
Let's sing the praises of ignorance.
Don't look at the potholes in your path:
bring back instead the times of yore!
Practice harder till you master
the skill of always walking backwards.
Let not a single thought of the present
break your focus upon the past!
Repeat the same thing over and over –

over and over, say only this:
How glorious was India in the past!
How sublime was India in days gone by!
Then, dear friends, you will arrive
and get to heaven after all.
Yep. We've been there for a while now.
Once you are there,
once you're in the same hell-hole,
keep in touch and tell us how it goes!

(Translation by Shabana Mir)

I

On 23 June 2017, Junaid (age 15) was anxiously waiting to celebrate Eid with a lot of gaiety with his family. He was on a train from Delhi to Mathura. Some men on the train began to mock him and his friends for their religion. They tugged at their beards and accused them of being beef eaters. The train compartment was crowded. Then the men attacked Junaid and his friends viciously. None of the co-passengers came to their rescue. Junaid was stabbed. Then the men pushed Junaid and his friends onto the platform at Asaoti railway station. Junaid bled to death in his brother's lap.

The men were arrested, but then released on bail. The wheels of justice are stuck. Junaid's mother waits for something to happen. But what was actually going to happen startled her. The key accused in the case attempted to contest the 2019 elections. This is what the key accused in such lynching cases do – they become politicians.

Numbness is creeping into society. These killings have become normal. So have all the other instances of intimidation, violence, expulsion, and coercion. This young boy was lynched in broad daylight just because he prayed to a different god. His story is now woven into the tapestry of India's history. It should not be forgotten.

Five children in Aligarh district (Uttar Pradesh) attacked a Dalit boy (age 12) in 2018 because – they said – he touched some balloons used for decorations on Janmashtami. When the boy touched the balloons, said his friend Suraj, the other children beat him to death. His mother – Savitri Devi – works as a labourer. She rushed to the hospital to find her son already dead. The village pradhan – Shyam Sunder Upadhyaya – did not, as it turns out, take the incident seriously. Nor did the media, which largely ignored it.

At *IndiaSpend*, Alison Saldanha, Pranav Rajput and Jay Hazare wrote in mid-2018 that until 2012, there was only one mob attack on 'child-lifting rumours' and since January 2017 there have been at least 69 such attacks with 33 people killed. The 'child-lifting rumour' is simple: a story goes around that a Muslim or a Dalit man has taken a child from a dominant caste community. A mob gathers and attacks any Muslim or Dalit man. This is the mentality that is sweeping the country. The authors quote from Upneet Lalli, the deputy director of the Institute for Correctional Administration in Chandigarh, 'The violence started with cow-related vigilantism, but it is now building up more violent behaviour – from small to big reasons, anything could be the trigger.' The figures collected by the authors are only indicative. The actual numbers are likely to be far higher.

The loudspeaker unites India and Pakistan. In Dadri, about 50 kilometres from Delhi, in 2015, two boys used the local temple's loudspeaker to mobilize a mob to protect cows and punish beef eaters. They accused Mohammed Akhlaq (age 52) of stealing a cow and slaughtering it. The mob beat Akhlaq and his son Danish (age 22). The father died, the son was badly injured. No one was prosecuted. It turned out that the meat in the family's refrigerator was mutton, not beef – although this has nothing to do with the crime of mob lynching. It was irrelevant to the villagers that Akhlaq's family had lived beside them for seventy years, or that his son had grown up in the village with their own children.

When the police came to arrest the men from the mob, the villagers stoned the police vehicles. The lynch mob – and the village, it seems – had forgotten all their cherished relations. They had finally discovered the 'enemy', and he needed to be punished. They had no memory of how in the sacred scriptures of the Hindus there is a dilemma posed to Arjun before war, that the warrior-archer hesitates when he must fight his own brethren, that he is anxious about the sacred battle (*dharm yudh*). None of that stayed the hand of the men who came when the loudspeaker called them.

The lynching of Akhlaq is mirrored across the border in Pakistan. In 2014, the people of Kot Radhakishan, a few hundred kilometres from Dadri, heard a call to violence from a loudspeaker mounted on a mosque. They were told that a Christian couple – Shama and Shahzad Masih – had desecrated the Quran. The mob dragged them out of where they had gone to hide, beat them and threw them – perhaps alive – into a brick kiln. It turned out later that the Masihs had not torn the Quran but had a dispute with the local brick kiln owner.

The Masihs were accused of blasphemy. So was Mashal Khan, a journalism student at Khan Abdul Wali Khan University in Mardan (Khyber Pakhtunkhwa, Pakistan). He was a bright young man who liked to discuss the writings of Karl Marx and Che Guevara as well as to think critically about religion. On 13 April 2017, Mashal Khan was grabbed by a mob, stripped, beaten and shot in the head and chest. He died soon after. The entire incident was videotaped and circulated on social media. The state tried 57 people, sentencing the main killer to death.

On one side of the border, 'blasphemy' is the excuse for mob violence, while on the other side it is 'cow protection'. In both countries, the state has offered legitimacy through laws against blasphemy and for the protection of cows. These laws go against basic human principles. They are used not necessarily by the state institutions, but by mobs that see themselves as defenders of both state laws and the laws of God. They fear nothing – neither the police nor their own moral compass. They are so sure that their violence is divine.

The numbers of those killed for blasphemy and the cow are outrageous. The Centre for Social Justice (Lahore, Pakistan) says that at least 62 men and women have been killed on suspicion of blasphemy between 1987 and 2015. This is conservative figure. India has seen more lynchings in the past four years.

Harishankar Parsai (1924-1995), the great satirist, said in the early 1960s, *the cow gives milk elsewhere; here it gives votes.* Both the cow and blasphemy are useful to the powerful. They allow them to mobilize populations for political purposes, without having to actually deal with the real issues that are in front of these people. The mobs in both Dadri and Kot Radhakishan suffer from hunger and unemployment, but these are not the issues that galvanize them. They are fired up to kill to defend norms that address none of their real issues.

II

Southern trees bear a strange fruit,
Blood on the leaves and blood at the root,
Black bodies swinging in the southern breeze,
Strange fruit hanging from the poplar trees.

The word lynching conjures up images of a dark period in the history of the United States of America. Between 1877 and 1950, white supremacist gangs murdered 4,000 African Americans, while the government and the police looked the other way. James Baldwin, whose essays in *Dark Days* capture the unfolding violence, wrote, 'A mob is not autonomous. It executes the real will of the people who rule the State.' In 1888, white supremacists lynched seven African American men for drinking from a well – which they had said was for 'whites only'. Baldwin recounts that story and writes, 'The blood is on the hands of the state of Alabama which sent those mobs into the street to execute the will of the State.'

The lyrics quoted above are from the iconic song – *Strange Fruit* – written by the communist artist Abel Meeropol and sung by Billie Holiday.

Lynching in India is not so far away from the American South. The sudden eruption of lynching events in the second decade of the 21st century is related to the ascent of majoritarian forces in India's polity and society. One of the first cases of lynching in this wave of murders took place less than a fortnight after the swearing in of the Modi government. Mohsin Mohammed Sheikh (age 28) worked as an information technology manager. On 4 June 2014, he was returning home with his friend when a gang associated with the *Hindu Rashtra Sena* – led by Dhananjay Desai – blocked his path and began to hit him with hockey sticks. It was later discovered that the assailants had been agitated over one of Mohsin Mohammed Sheikh's Facebook posts. He was killed on the spot. It was the first communally-targeted killing in Modi-led India.

Despite the controversial record of the Sena in the police files, and despite the fact that the Maharashtra government had once contemplated banning the group, the High Court judge – Mridula Bhatkar – granted bail to the three men accused of killing Mohsin Sheikh. The order given by the judge is remarkable and deserves quotation:

> The applicants/accused otherwise had no other motive such as any personal enmity against the innocent deceased Mohsin. The fault of the deceased was only that he belonged to another religion. I consider this factor in favour of the applicants/accused. Moreover, the applicants/accused do not have criminal record and it appears that in the name of religion, they were provoked and have committed the murder. Under such circumstances, I allow the bail Applications.

In other words, if one kills someone out of personal enmity then that is worse than if someone is killed merely on religious grounds. Those who kill in the name of religion should be – by Justice Bhatkar's logic – given favourable treatment vis-à-vis other kinds of murder. The Supreme Court could not tolerate this judgment. It observed that the High Court ruling was 'coloured with bias for or against a community'. It set aside the order of the Bombay High Court. The rot had run deep. Even a High Court judge could take the view that killing in the name of religion was not deeply awful and unlawful.

Lynching appeared in India not as individual acts – one person killing another – but as group violence – mobs targeting religious minorities, Dalits, transgender persons and people from a variety of deprived sections. Anyone considered 'other' was fair game. Professor Sanjay Subrahmanyam, who teaches at the University of California, Los Angeles, told *The Indian Express* that the members of lynch mobs know that nothing will happen to them, that their acts have the approval of higher authorities.

Earlier, organized acts of mass violence were repetitive in character and there was a pattern, e.g. processions were attacked, or the violence was timed with public festivals. This was so even in the time of the Mughals. Then, post-Independence, there have been largely urban, organized forms of violence, where various political parties have provided protection to the perpetrators.

The difference between the earlier phase of mass violence and the current phrase required further differentiation. Professor Subrahmanyam continued,

> But what we are seeing now is not at a single place, there are fewer numbers attacked and it is decentralized, done by little groups all over the place. These groups are either being told or imagine that they have been told to act in this way. Further, after the event, no one in authority is clearly telling them the contrary. There is also an aspirational quality to the violence. . . . [The] curious thing is that the perpetrators want it to be known. After all, some of the people doing this are even videotaping it. They make sure the information is circulating, intended as a warning, as a signal and controlling device for the social behaviour expected of minorities. It is a form of violence which can pop up here one day and there on another. It is never mass killings but based on the existence of grassroots kind of organizations which believe in doing this, and also to an extent on copycat behaviour. So even if it is decentralized, there is a larger context.

If anyone doubts this dynamic, then it is worthwhile to look at the excerpts of a sting operation done by NDTV regarding the killing of a meat trader – Qasim Qureshi – in Hapur (Uttar Pradesh) and the beating of Samiuddin. The police arrested Yudhishthir Singh Sisodia who was the main accused. Let off on bail, Sisodia spoke to NDTV's A. Vaidyanathan, who had a hidden camera. Sisodia told the court that he had no role in the killing, but when Vaidyanathan asked him about it, he said,

> I told the jailer that [the victims] were slaughtering cows, so I slaughtered them. My army is ready. If anyone slaughters a cow, we will kill them and go to jail a thousand times.

III

The New India of the BJP is a normal of hatred and bigotry. This new normal is an unholy alliance of corporate interests and Hindutva zealots. It is defined by upturning the rule of law, sabotage of institutions, and the creation of an atmosphere of fear. India has become a republic of fear instead of a republic of hope. It is worthwhile following Aarti Sethi's question about how certain deaths become 'non-events'. She has in mind the murder of Junaid Khan.

In *The Indian Express*, Kaunain Sheriff M. returned to the railway station in Faridabad to find out who saw what when Junaid was killed. He found that nobody *saw* anything as a young boy lay bleeding to death on platform number 4. The blood stains, the journalist writes, were 'still visible' on the platform and yet no one saw anything, neither the Station Master Om Prakash nor the Post-Master Bhagwat Dyal whose office is right across from the platform. 'I did not see anything,' said Om Prakash. 'I did not see anything,' said Bhagwat Dyal. They used the same sentence. Even the CCTV did not see anything. One official said, 'There is a CCTV camera opposite the spot. The wire has been tampered with and it is non-functional.' Sethi recounts what she read from Sheriff M. and writes,

> Then they collectively, and without prior agreement, continued to not see what they had seen after the event. This is the uniquely terrifying aspect of this incident on which this report reflects: the totalizing force of an unspoken, but collectively binding, agreement between Hindus to not see the dead body of a Muslim child. Hindus on this railway platform in a small station in north India instantly produced a stranger sociality, a common social bond between people who do not otherwise know each other. By mutual recognition

between strangers, Hindus at this platform agreed to abide by a code of silence by which the death of a Muslim child cannot be seen by 200 people in full public view on a railway platform in today's India.

Based on this blindness, Sethi offers two main considerations:

1. We are in a radical breakdown of the rule of law in BJP-ruled India and in these regions mob rule now obtains. We are in the terror days of state supported goondaraj. From which flows the second conclusion.
2. On the 22nd of June 2017, the Republic effectively ended. India is no longer a secular constitutional republic but on the precipice of being transformed into a majoritarian State ruled by an ethnic and religious majority.

The lynching of Junaid was not seen by two hundred people who were on the platform at that time. They did not see the violence. They did not see Junaid. This can be contrasted to the response of Ian Grillot (age 24) when a gunman came to kill Srinivas Kuchibhotla and Alok Madasani in a bar in Olathe, Kansas (USA) in 2017. Grillot put himself in the line of fire, shot in the chest as he attempted to stop the shooter killing more people (Kuchibhotla died later of his wounds). When Ian Grillot was hailed as a hero, he said, 'I was just doing what anyone should have done for another human being. It's not about where he was from or his ethnicity. We're all humans. I just felt I did what was naturally right to do.' If he had not acted, he said, he could not have 'lived with myself if I wouldn't have stopped or attempted to stop the shooter'.

In Portland, Oregon (USA) in 2017, a white man shouted racist slurs at two girls – one of whom wore a hijab. Three men on that train intervened. Two died – Ricky John Best (age 53) and Taliesin Myrddin Namkai-Meche (age 23). The third man – Micah David-Cole Fletcher (age 21) was badly wounded. Namkai-Meche's mother – Asha Deliverance – said of her son, 'My dear baby boy passed on yesterday while protecting two young Muslim girls from a racist man on the train in Portland. Shining bright star, I love you forever.'

The two hundred people on the platform in Asaoti were not suffering from the kind of ethical dilemma that drove Ian Grillot to action, or that drove Best and Namkai-Meche to their deaths.

IV

The rule of law slips into mob violence.

The element of surprise has now vanished. It is rightly said that these days it is difficult to distinguish between vigilante mob violence and the violence of the state. When a mob attacks under whatever pretext it can think of, the police – the most visible of the state's arm – turns into a mute spectator or at times it even prods the attacks on. When Qasim Qureshi (age 45), the cattle trader, was lynched in Hapur in 2018, the police initially tried to cover up the murder as a case of road rage. On the video, some policemen were seen leading the mob as it dragged Qasim on the street. Thanks to a sting operation by a television channel, the Supreme Court has taken up the case and promises urgent action. This is only one of many examples that illustrates the close collaboration between the police and the mobs.

One key example of the entanglement of the state and the mob is the forcible closure of a popular hotel – Hayat Rabbani – in Jaipur on 19 March 2017. The Mayor of the Jaipur Municipal Corporation – Ashok Lahoty – contributed to a spurious rumour by forwarding a message to a WhatsApp group of the BJP media cell. This message said that the hotel was 'feeding beef to cows' by dumping beef in the garbage area. It called for 'holy action' against the hotel. Kamal Didi, the national president of the *Rashtriya Mahila Gau Raksha Dal* – one of the cow vigilante groups, brought about 150 people to protest after they heard these rumours. They caught two people who worked at the hotel. These two hotel employees were thrashed by the mob, a mob incited by an elected official. Naeem Rabbani, the owner of the hotel, said that his staff had just eaten a chicken dinner. There was no beef, as validated by the Forensic Science Laboratory. This did not stop the hand of the Mayor or of the Sadhvi.

The Mayor sent another WhatsApp message – 'Hotel Hayat has been seized for daring to feed beef to cows'. 'The owners do not have permission to run a hotel,' he told Hamza Khan of *The Indian Express*. 'They do not have permission to run a restaurant.' The courts did not agree. An additional civil judge gave an injunction that the hotel be allowed to reopen. The additional sessions judge had to send his *naazir* (head assistant) to the hotel to break the locks and open the seal.

The entire phenomenon of cow vigilantes that burst onto the Indian scene during the first few years of Modi's prime ministership has a prehistory in the violence against Dalits over the issue of the cow and cow slaughter.

In 2002, a mob of about a thousand people in the town of Dulina, Jhajjar (Haryana) killed five Dalits. The reason given was that the Dalits had skinned a dead cow (although the rumour that spread was that there was an incident of 'cow slaughter by Muslims'). The mob thrashed the men in front of a police station, in the presence of senior officers of the administration. The police lodged a case not against the mob and its leaders but against the dead people for 'provoking the people'. The victims become the perpetrators and the perpetrators become the martyrs. The killers came to the police with large crowds. They were cheered on by the crowds. The lynching was called a *gohatya kand* not a *Dalit hatyakand*, the killing of cows not the killing of Dalits.

A People's Union of Democratic Rights report from 2003 (*Dalit Lynching at Dulina: Cow Protection, Caste and Communalism*) reported that the VHP and the Shiv Sena held a demonstration in Jhajjar and told the Deputy Commissioner that no action should be taken against the killers. They glorified the killers as heroes who had avenged the death of 'our mother', the cow. VHP leader Parmanand Giri said that the killers of the *gau hatyare* 'must be honoured'. The killers were seen by these Hindutva fanatics as 'religious warriors', not as murderers.

In March 2016, Mustain Abbas (age 27) was killed in Kurukshetra district by cow vigilante groups. The High Court of Punjab and Haryana looked into this case on a petition from Abbas's father Tahir Hasan. The court offered an interim order that said that the police and the district administration failed to do their constitutional duty. The judges wrote,

> So called vigilante groups so constituted with the backing of political bosses and senior functionaries governing the State including police under the name and style of Gau Raksha Dal has sought to take the law in its own hands. The local administration, be it the police or otherwise, by their muteness and connivance are allowing unleashing terror upon the persons carrying on such a trade in animals. (*Tahir Hasan v. State of Haryana & Ors.*, CRWP No. 382 of 2016, High Court of Punjab and Haryana, 18 March 2016.)

No equivocation here. The court is clear. There is the smell of deep collusion between the political establishment and the cow vigilante mobs. It only emboldens the vigilantes when the government frames new cow slaughter rules – Prevention of Cruelty to Animals (Regulation of Livestock Markets) Rule of 2017

– that effectively ban cow slaughter. The 'sacredness of the cow' makes it appear as if human flesh is less important than bovine flesh, that the cow is more important than the human.

It is not just cow vigilantes. There are many kinds of vigilantes. There are vigilantes against love. The elopement of a girl from one community with a boy from another has fuelled the discourse of 'love jihad', leading to the forcible expulsion of families from a region and the death of the young people – all with police collusion. There are the vigilantes against freedom, with any talk of human rights in Kashmir – for example – raising the ire of the mobsters, who act against those whom they call 'anti-national' with the full backing of the police.

V

The new 'normal' has created new 'heroes'.

Jaipur's Kamal Didi, who led the attack on the Hayat Rabbani Hotel compared the alleged killers of Pehlu Khan (age 55), a Muslim dairy farmer from Haryana, by a band of cow vigilantes to Bhagat Singh, Sukhdev and Chandrasekhar Azad. There is a vast gap between Bhagat Singh, Sukhdev and Azad, the iconic freedom fighters against British colonialism, and the killers of Pehlu Khan. When one of the alleged killers – Vipin Yadav – met the Sadhvi Kamal Didi, she said to him, 'The entire country is with you.' These are the heroes of the Hindutva fanatics.

In December 2017, Shambhu Lal Regar hacked Afrazul Khan – a Muslim worker – to death in Rajsamand (Rajasthan) and later burned him. Regar says he killed Khan to prevent an act of 'love jihad', where a Muslim man might seduce a Hindu woman. The brutal act was filmed. It circulated on WhatsApp groups around Rajsamand. It then spread through the country. The act should have been condemned by everyone. But it was not. Hundreds of people – many associated with the Bajrang Dal – came onto the streets to hail Regar as a hero. They fought the police and injured thirty policemen. They mobbed the court and raised Rs. 2.5 lakhs for Regar. A BJP state office bearer put a picture of Regar as his profile picture on WhatsApp. During Ramnavmi celebrations in Jodhpur, he was honoured with a tableau in which he sits on a throne-like chair with a pickaxe in his hand. A banner above the tableau reads, 'Hindu brethren to protect their sisters and daughters and liberate the country from love jihad'.

The glorification of Regar is not the first incident of its kind, although the glorification was given a boost by the right-wing government at the Centre.

In 1999, Graham Staines, a pastor who worked to eradicate leprosy in Odisha, and his two children – Philip and Timothy – were burnt to death in Manoharpur by a group of fifty fanatics led by Ravinder Pal (Dara Singh). This murderer – Dara Singh – had also been charged with the killing of a Muslim trader Shaikh Rehman and a Christian cleric Arul Das. He was convicted by the courts and sentenced to life imprisonment. Shambhu was portrayed as a 'symbol of Hindu anger'. False fears of conversion were peddled as the rationale for the killing of Staines, his children as well as Rehman and Das. Many groups emerged to defend Dara Singh and to continue his work. Terror is their business.

A glance through the newspapers these days finds the stories of many such violent acts and many fanatics made into heroes.

Hundreds of people gathered at the Nashik and Pune court-houses to sprinkle rose petals on the Malegaon bombers, the terror cell that comprised of gurus, retired and active military officers and their various associates. The nexus of this cell came to light thanks to the tireless efforts of Hemant Karkare, the Mumbai Anti-Terror Squad chief.

On 11 October 2007, just before *Iftar*, a bomb exploded at the Ajmer Sharif Dargah, a Sufi shrine that was visited by Muslims and

Hindus alike. The National Investigation Agency found two people – both ex-pracharaks of the RSS – Sunil Joshi and Lokesh Sharma to be the main conspirators. They found Bhavesh Patel to be guilty of planting explosives at the Dargah. The plan was to kill as many people as possible. Hundreds of people gathered for prayers. Two people died. Patel's sentence was suspended by the High Court and he was released on bail. When Bhavesh Patel returned home to Bharuch in 2018 he was given a grand welcome. Patel was carried through the large crowd on the shoulders of various people. BJP's Surbhiben Tamakuwala, president of the Bharuch municipality, and Marutisinh Atodariya, a councillor, as well as Viral Desai of the VHP and various RSS members were in attendance.

Valorization of fanatics has become the rule rather than the exception. Those who kill rationalists and journalists, Dalits and Muslims are celebrated in the circles of the right wing. This is the case across South Asia. The grave of Mumtaz Qadri, the assassin of the Punjab (Pakistan) Governor Salman Taseer, has become a shrine. Thousands of people visit it each week. Taseer had defended a working-class Christian woman who was charged with blasphemy. That is why Qadri killed him. When Qadri went to court, rose petals were sprinkled on him and about three hundred lawyers appeared to represent him pro bono.

When the journalist Gauri Lankesh was killed, the world of Twitter exploded with both anger and grief, but also – in the sewers of the right-wing – in joy. Former Zee TV journalist Jagrati Shukla wrote, 'So Commy Gauri Lankesh has been murdered mercilessly. Your deeds always come back to haunt you, they say. Amen.' A businessman from Gujarat – Nikhil Dadhich – called Gauri Lankesh a 'bitch'. He is a trader from Surat. His Twitter account is 'honoured to be followed by PM Sh. @narendramodi Ji', he writes. His other followers include Union Minister Giriraj Singh and BJP North Gujarat media cell-in-charge Parag Sheth.

The lionization of the killers does not remain in the present.

It goes into the past. Nathuram Godse, who killed Gandhi, has become a person of reverence – for public valorization – amongst the fanatics and the right wing. 'Godse was God sent', 'Gandhi should have been hanged', 'Godse had valid reason to shoot Gandhi', and 'I'm a big Godse fan, so what?' – those are the kind of messages that clutter the internet. Temples are built for Godse. In April 2006, two fanatics died as they made their bombs in Nanded. It turned out that they celebrated the day of Godse's death as Hutatma (Martyr) Day. They are not the only ones to do so. It is a practice amongst the right wing. Godse is joined by those who attacked the Babri Masjid in 1992 and those who have assassinated journalists and Muslims, activists and Dalits. One of the chief architects of the attack on the Babri Masjid has been celebrated as Hindu Hriday Samrat (Emperor of Hindu Hearts).

The normalization of violence against innocent people and the valorization of their killers raises serious questions about the moral compass of our societies. Writing of Adolf Eichmann, the Nazi who organized the Holocaust, the philosopher Hannah Arendt wrote,

> The trouble with Eichmann was precisely that so many were like him, and that the many were neither perverted nor sadistic, that they were, and still are, terribly and terrifyingly normal. From the viewpoint of our legal institutions and of our moral standards of judgment, this normality was much more terrifying than all the atrocities put together.

VI

> A few gave the appearance of being truly psychopathic individuals. The mass of others were ragged and illiterate peasants easily roused to hatred of the Tutsis. Perhaps the most sinister people I met were the educated political elite, men and women of charm

> and sophistication who spoke flawless French and who could engage in long philosophical debates about the nature of war and democracy. But they shared one thing in common with the soldiers and the peasants: They were drowning in the blood of their fellow countrymen.

Fergal Keane, a BBC journalist, wrote these lines in his book *Season of Blood: A Rwandan Journey.* It sends a chill down one's spine. The organized and planned killing in Rwanda resulted in the death of eight lakh Tutsis in 1994. It was one of the darkest episodes of the last decade of the 20th century.

The echoes from Rwanda to India are loud.

Violence is a fact of life in India. Surely this violence must be blamed both on the perpetrators of violence, the fanatics on the streets, and on the deep social roots that generate this violence.

In the late 1970s and 1980s, during our student days, one could always see that after a riot sensitive people would hold 'communal harmony' rallies. This would lead to the view that fanatics were only a few bad apples who would disturb an essential harmony. Looking back to those days, one feels the innocence of our views. We talked through the day and into the night about the tolerance of our great culture and we kept patting ourselves on the back, refusing to see the routinization and normalization of violence in our society. We would take shelter behind the greatness of the apostle of non-violence – Gandhi – and yet not consider how one terrible type of violence had become legitimate: the kind of violence that was used against Dalits, women and other oppressed sections of society.

This violence had religious sanction for centuries and the emergence of Indian modernity – through the freedom movement – had not delegitimized this sanction. Rather, the toxicity of these hierarchical customs that grew out of caste society and of Hinduism swamped Islam, Christianity and Buddhism within India.

Imagine the kind of violence. A woman whose husband dies is burnt alive on her dead husband's funeral pyre. If earlier female infanticide was practised as part of a culture of misogyny, now sex-selective abortion is utilized to do the same thing. There are 33 million missing women in India. Where have they gone? These are facts that need to be looked at directly, not discarded in the name of 'tolerance'. Dr. Ambedkar did not shy away from this violence. A reading of his work makes it clear how this violence is ingrained in our society. Dr. Ambedkar points out that when the priests deny a Dalit entry into a temple or when a Dalit is thrashed for reading the Vedas, these acts are not seen as illegal but as the observation of a religious duty. Religion, it is said, enjoins the person to humiliate Dalits. This is the code of conduct of the religion, even if it violates the code of conduct of the Constitution.

Is a communal riot legitimate or illegitimate? Laws on the books are not a barometer to help answer this question. The acts of the state are a clearer indication. The Bureau of Police Research and Development – a Union Home Ministry body – released a study that showed that between 1954 and 1996, there were 21,000 incidents of rioting with 16,000 dead and a lakh of people injured. What is important about this study is that it shows that only a handful of people were held accountable for the violence and deaths. Many of those who should be held accountable are – as in Rwanda – part of the 'educated political elite, men and women of charm and sophistication'. None of them see the inside of a prison cell.

A citizenry that is opposed to terrorism exhibits a strange sense of ambivalence towards this kind of indiscriminate violence and arson. Studies show that these riots are hardly spontaneous – the work of frustrated people – and are much more organized affairs. Political scientist Paul R. Brass describes an 'institutionalized riot system' that produces these acts of great violence. In his study of Meerut (2004), Brass defines this system in the following way:

> Far from being spontaneous occurrences, the production of such riots involves calculated and deliberate actions by key individuals, the conveying of messages, recruitment of participants, and other specific types of activities, especially provocative ones, that are part of a performative repertoire. Moreover, all these actions may require frequent rehearsals until the time is ripe, the context is felicitous, and there are no serious obstructions in carrying out the performance.

Court cases are often dismissed because the perpetrators of the violence claim that they had no role in it because the mayhem was 'spontaneous'. This is a spurious defence, but it works. It worked for the killers in Nellie (Assam) and in Delhi.

On 18 February 1983, armed mobs in Nagaon in central Assam killed between 3,000 and 10,000 people – mainly Muslims – over the course of six hours. Why did they conduct this massacre? They claimed that the people whom they killed had come from Bangladesh without documents. There was an entire political story to the killing, which had to do with the electoral clash between the All-Assam Students Union and the Congress party. But that was only part of the story. The main element here is that all these decades later, the report of the inquiry commission, headed by T.P. Tiwari, on the violence – submitted a quarter century ago (1984) – remains unattended. There are only three copies of this report. No political party in Assam today wants to revisit the massacre. No one wants to pressure the government to publish the Tiwari commission report. When a Japanese scholar – Makiko Kimura – wanted to present a paper on the Nellie Massacre at the Omeo Kumar Das Institute in Guwahati (Assam), she was denied permission. No reason was given to her. Kimura had done extensive research in Nellie in 2001. Her paper was about the three different narratives of the cause of the massacre. It did not point any fingers. Even then, she was not allowed to open the subject. The government wants it to be closed.

Silence has shrouded the Delhi massacre of 1984, when at least three thousand Sikhs were killed in the aftermath of the assassination of Prime Minister Indira Gandhi. But then, in December 2018, the Delhi High Court – led by Justice S. Muralidhar and Justice Vinod Goel – ruled in *State Through CBI v. Sajjan Kumar and Ors.*, that not only were senior Congress party leaders involved in the mass killing but that there was a 'familiar pattern' to the murders:

> There has been a familiar pattern of mass killings in Mumbai in 1993, in Gujarat in 2002, in Kandhamal, Odisha in 2008, in Muzaffarnagar in U.P. in 2013 to name a few.
>
> Common to these mass crimes were the targeting of minorities and the attacks spearheaded by the dominant political actors being facilitated by the law enforcement agencies. The criminals responsible for the mass crimes have enjoyed political patronage and managed to evade prosecution and punishment.

Bringing such criminals to justice poses a serious challenge to our legal system. As these appeals themselves demonstrate, decades pass by before they can be made answerable. This calls for strengthening the legal system. Neither 'crimes against humanity' nor 'genocide' is part of our domestic law of crime. This loophole needs to be addressed urgently.

VII

How far India has travelled from the hopes of the freedom movement, to some extent captured by the 'Tryst with Destiny' spirit!

In August 2018, the Punjab government attempted to amend the Indian Penal Code to make criticism of religious books an act of sacrilege and to consider this a major offence. Such a move would introduce provisions that would undermine what remains of the secular character of the Constitution. A civil society group – Constitutional Conduct – wrote a letter to the Punjab Chief Minister Amarinder Singh and to Congress president Rahul Gandhi to contest this move. They say that instead of 'reducing the role of religion from matters of the State, this move will further consolidate the hold of sectarianism, and strengthen the hands of religious extremists on all sides'. Constitutional Conduct, made up largely of retired civil servants, wrote that blasphemy laws are 'a direct threat to freedom of speech and expression'. Such laws, they note, are misused around the world, mainly used 'against minorities and weaker sections to harass them, exact revenge and also to settle personal and professional quarrels – all matters entirely unrelated to blasphemy'.

A discussion of the tarnished spirit of secularism and socialism would have to include the proposed amendment to the Citizenship Act of 1955 as discussed earlier.

The discussion would need to include moves to not only legitimize 'Hindu rituals in the public sphere', as the journalist Bharat Bhushan put it, but also to 'create a predominantly Hindutva public sphere that marginalizes others'. Mythology has slipped in to undermine science. In 2016, talking about Rajasthan, *India Today* reported,

> Since 1st July 2015, yoga, pranayam, vande mataram, surya namaskar and meditation have been made compulsory at the time of school prayers; Saraswati Puja worship has been made compulsory in every government and non-government school on Basant Panchami; a school development committee has been formed in every school and its meeting is compulsory on every *Amavasya* (no moon day); *Bhagwadgeeta* has been made part of curriculum; and

> Geeta and Jail diary of Bhagat Singh have been made mandatory in schools. Books on Integral Humanism and Samajik Samarasta have been made part of school libraries.

A leading scientist, G. Madhavan Nair (former chairperson of the Indian Space Research Organisation) offered the theory that the *shlokas* in the Vedas mentioned the presence of water on the moon. 'The Vedas had a lot of information in the field of space and atomic energy,' he said. 'We were fine until 600 BC. Then came the time of invasions till independence.' The timeline is significant. Madhavan Nair is pointing a finger at a communal historiography, one which blames 'Muslims' for the degeneration of India.

What happened to India's secular ethos? Secularism used to be thought of as 'equality for all religions' (*Sarv dharm sambhav*), a Gandhian idea. But against this idea came the more liberal formulation to separate religion from politics. There is an absence of clarity in the discussions in India. After the Hindutva supremacists demolished the Babri Masjid in 1992, there was a section of the progressives that called for the appropriation of a 'real Ram' against a 'phoney Ram', the play – in other words – of the game of good religion versus bad religion.

Serious thought was not given to the whole process of secularization, which the Marxist critic Peter Berger defined as 'a process by which sectors of society and culture are removed from the domination of religious institutions and symbols'. If a society is not secular, what is the point of focusing in on making the state secular? Should the focus not be on the secularization of society? Perhaps there was a sense that with the process of industrialization, religion will decline, that in the interim it was important to have a secular state? Meera Nanda suggests that the Enlightenment Project 'believed that as men and women begin to understand the underlying order of nature without involving God, they will learn to outgrow their faith in God'. The Indian Constitution is based on this classical view of secularization. Our confidence in the rationalization of the work process would remove all space for the ideas of divine intervention and magical action.

Meanwhile, in society, the space was open for all kinds of reactionary interventions by communal forces.

Secularism was seen largely as part of an anti-communal struggle, not seen broadly as a fight to empty 'religion from autonomous social spaces', as the philosopher Charles Taylor put it. Movements that were not directly related to 'communal forces' had nonetheless a major role to play in the secularization of society. Amongst these movements one must include the anti-caste or Dalit movement, the movements against patriarchy and gender-based oppression, the people's science movement, the rationalist movement and the movement of the exploited and the oppressed for dignity and rights. These are essential parts of the movement to secularize society, to take us away from lynchistan.

THREE. *SACRED COWS*

> It is a curious people. With them, all life seems to be sacred except human life.
>
> – Mark Twain, *Following the Equator*, 1897

> To the question whether the Hindus ever ate beef, every Touchable Hindu, whether he is a Brahmin or a non-Brahmin, will say 'no, never'. In a certain sense, he is right. From times no Hindu has eaten beef. If this is all that the Touchable Hindu wants to convey by his answer there need be no quarrel over it. But when the learned Brahmins argue that the Hindus not only never ate beef but they always held the cow to be sacred and were always opposed to the killing of the cow, it is impossible to accept their view.
>
> – B.R. Ambedkar, 'Did the Hindus Never Eat Beef?', *The Untouchables*, 1948

I

Did the Hindus never eat beef? Dr. B.R. Ambedkar dealt with this specific issue in a number of his texts, most clearly in *The Untouchables* (1948).

The saffron fanatics are keen to appropriate Ambedkar, but what they do not realize or what they would like to disguise is his deep appeal to fight both Brahminism and capitalism. Ambedkar goes to the root of Indian history to understand the emergence of hierarchies based on caste. He, unlike the saffron intellectuals, has no interest in the fallacious blame given to Islam for the deep roots of caste in the country. There is a world of difference between the ideas of Hindutva and the ideas of Ambedkar.

The saffron intellectuals are keen to offer a sanitized version of Ambedkar, his radical views left out. He is put on the same saffron pedestal that holds such RSS heroes as Savarkar, Golwalkar and Hedgewar. These are men that the saffron intellectuals say are worth remembering in the morning (*pratah smaraniya*). They gloss over the important points made by Ambedkar that are deeply critical of Hinduism and of Hindutva. In the mid-1930s, Ambedkar said that he 'may be born a Hindu' but he 'would not die a Hindu'. This is just what he did in 1956, when he converted to Buddhism along with lakhs of his followers. In his *Pakistan or the Partition of India* (1945), Ambedkar wrote,

> If Hindu Raj does becomes a fact, it will no doubt, be the greatest calamity for this country. No matter what the Hindus say, Hinduism is a menace to liberty, equality and fraternity. On that account it is incompatible with democracy. Hindu Raj must be prevented at any cost.

The saffron intellectuals want to downplay all this and to promote Ambedkar as a Hindu social reformer, so as to fool the Dalit masses. Or so they think.

The selective amnesia of the saffron intellectuals is not limited only to the figure of someone as important as Ambedkar. Even people like Swami Vivekanand are far more complex than the Sangh and its outfits would acknowledge. Like Ambedkar, Swami Vivekanand held views on beef far divergent from the narrow views of the RSS and its clique. In Pasadena, California (USA), Swami Vivekanand addressed the Shakespeare Club on 2 February 1900. The theme was 'Buddhistic India'. He said, 'You will be astonished if I tell you that, according to old ceremonials, he is not a good Hindu who does not eat beef. On certain occasions he must sacrifice a bull and eat it.' Swami Vivekanand's Ramakrishna Mission sponsored research on key questions of the Indian past. One of the texts, by the scholar Chittenjoor Kunhan Raja, on the Vedas, reflected on the food of the ancient world:

> The Vedic Aryans, including the Brahmanas, ate fish, meat and even beef. A distinguished guest was honoured with beef served at a meal. Although the Vedic Aryans ate beef, milch cows were not killed. One of the words that designated cow was *aghnya* (what shall not be killed). But a guest was a *goghna* (one for whom a cow is killed). It is only bulls, barren cows and calves that were killed.

V.D. Savarkar, the pioneer of the concept of Hindutva, bluntly writes in his book *Ksha-Kirane* (1936) that 'the cow is neither God nor mother but purely a useful animal. We should not worship it but we must breed and nurture the animal because we can reap the best advantages from it'. This text is quite harsh in its tone. Savarkar says that if an animal is worth worshipping, then why not worship the pig? There are references, he said, from the Vedas of cow slaughter ('*Gomedhhi vedadikat turalakpane ullekhile aahe*'). In *Samaj Chitre*, Savarkar wrote,

> Animals such as the cow and buffalo and trees such as banyan and peepal are useful to man, hence we are fond of them; to that extent we might even consider them worthy of worship! . . . Does it not follow then that when under certain circumstances, that animal or tree becomes a source of trouble to mankind, it ceases to be worthy of sustenance or protection and as such its destruction is in humanitarian or national interests and becomes a human or national dharma?

All of this is buried by the saffron intellectuals. For them, silence serves the purpose (*maunam sarvatra sadhanam*). It is why the RSS hates the work of Dr. Dwijendra Narayan Jha, whose book *The Myth of the Holy Cow*, lays out the actual history of food in ancient India. Jha uses evidence from Brahminical, Buddhist and Jain religious texts to dispel the myth that the killing of the cow and eating of its flesh was introduced into India by the followers of Islam. He says that ancient Indians ate beef much before the entry of Islam into India. In an interview, Jha says,

> Animal sacrifice was very common in the Vedic period. In the *agnadheya*, which was a preparatory rite preceding all public sacrifices, a cow was required to be killed. In the *asvamedha*, the most important of public sacrifices, more than 600 animals and birds were killed and its finale was marked by the sacrifice of 21 cows. In the *gosava*, an important component of public sacrifices like the rajasuya and the vajapeya, a cow was offered to Maruts. . . .

In his article 'Cow and the Elusive Hindu Identity', Jha writes,

> The evidence from the epics is unambiguous. Most of the characters in the *Mahabharata* are meat eaters, but what is more, it makes a laudatory reference to the King Rantideva in whose kitchen two thousand cows were butchered every day, their flesh, along with grains, being distributed among the brahmans. Similarly the *Ramayana* of Valmiki makes frequent reference to the killing of animals including the cow for sacrifice as well as food.

Jha is not alone. Nrisingha Prasad Bhaduri, a leading Indologist and expert in Vedic scriptures who heads the Netaji Institute for Asian Studies (Kolkata), writes, 'The Vedas encapsulate the essence of Hindu dharma. They are replete with instances of sages and even gods consuming beef. In fact, a guest in a Hindu household used to be referred to – according to the Vedas – as "*goghna*" or he who is served beef as part of the hospitality ritual.' Quoting the *Shatpath Brahman*, Bhaduri adds, 'Yajnavalkya – one of the earliest philosophers in recorded history – who questions many metaphysical propositions also says, *I eat it [beef] only if it is cooked till it is tender*. The king of the gods, Indra, too is said to be fond of beef. In the *Rig Veda*, Indra demands that he be served 15 to 20 cooked oxen.' Jha and Bhaduri are joined in this view by scholars such as D.D. Kosambi, P.V. Kane, Laxman Shastri Joshi and Rajendra Lal Mitra. These scholars wrote about beef eating and cow sacrifice as early as 1891 (Mitra in *The Indo-Aryans*, 1891), and through the 1940s (Kane in his monumental five-volume *History of Dharmasastra*).

II

> My brief was to prevent any ban on cow slaughter. It was important for us in the dairy business to keep weeding out the unhealthy cows so that available resources could be utilized for healthy and productive cattle. I was prepared to go as far as to allow that no useful cow should be killed. This was the point on which the Shankaracharya [of Puri] and I invariably locked horns and got into heated arguments. I constantly asked him, 'Your Holiness, are you going to take all the useless cows which are not producing anything and look after them and feed them till they die? You know that cannot work.' He never had any answer to my query.
>
> – Verghese Kurien, *I Too Had a Dream*, 2005

The BJP government likes to portray itself as cow friendly, as peopled by cow worshippers. To prove its credentials, it has even enacted fresh laws for the cow and has strengthened existing laws, as well as provided extra funds for the upkeep of cows. It has even established a ministry of cow welfare.

In the 1990s, the Shiv Sena-BJP government in Maharashtra pushed this issue to the front of the political agenda. They passed a bill called the Maharashtra Animal Preservation (Amendment) Bill of 1995, which banned the slaughter of bulls, bullocks and calves, in addition to cows. It remained with the President's office for around two decades.

When the BJP took power in Maharashtra just five months after Modi took office at the Centre, the government of Devendra Fadnavis (himself an RSS product) sought fresh Presidential assent to the said bill. President Pranab Mukherjee took no time to give the bill clearance.

The impact of this bill was immediately felt by 1.5 million people who worked in the cattle and meat industry – whether in the transportation of animals, the butchering of them, the processing of the meat or the distribution of the meat to markets inside and outside India. The impact was wider than this. It included the merchants who would sell the cattle and cow hide to tanneries as far off as Kolkata and Chennai, and the leather manufacturers in these centres. There was an impact on farmers, who would now tend to cattle which had lost its value. Impoverishment and desolation was the consequence. But the government did not care.

Maharashtra was not the only state to suddenly become active on the cow protection front. Other saffron-ruled states had the same kind of energy on cow protection, energy which they did not have for necessary pro-people measures (notably on the agrarian crisis).

In 2016, Haryana's BJP government led by Manohar Lal Khattar (another RSS man) gave licences to cow protection gangs, supposedly to help the police keep a check on alleged cow smuggling. The government set up a 24-hour helpline for citizens to report cow slaughter and smuggling. It appointed a police task force to respond to these complaints. Gujarat's BJP government of Anandiben Patel in March 2017 declared that cow slaughter was punishable by life imprisonment. Rajasthan's BJP government led by Vasundhara Raje imposed additional taxes in April 2017 on 'conservation and propagation of cow and its progeny'. The state had already created a department to ensure the welfare of cows. In March 2017, the BJP government in Uttar Pradesh led by Yogi Adityanath campaigned against 'illegal' slaughterhouses and meat shops.

Outside government, the cow protector groups – often with close ideological and organizational ties to the BJP and the RSS – fought to ban the killing of cows and to popularize this issue on the streets. One such group – the Bharatiya Gau Raksha Dal – is an umbrella organization that was set up in 2012. The network has about fifty groups across the country affiliated to it. There are at least 10,000 volunteers who operate in each state of the country. Pawan Pandit, its leader, told Human Rights Watch in 2017, 'Now the entire India is a cow protection group because people are angered by such cruelty to animals.' The BJP, he says, is not strong enough on the issue.

In 2019, Human Rights Watch released a report on 'Violent Cow Protection in India', in which it cited an NDTV survey that showed that there has been a nearly 500 per cent increase in the use of communal language in speeches by elected leaders – 90 per cent of them from the BJP – between 2014 and 2018 (this is compared to the five years before the BJP came to power). 'Cow protection,' notes the survey, 'formed an important theme in a number of speeches.'

III

In April 2017, BJP leader and Commerce Minister Nirmala Sitharaman spoke on a debate in the Lok Sabha on the availability of raw hide and skin for the leather industry after the ban on cow slaughter in Uttar Pradesh. Speaking on behalf of Uttar Pradesh's Chief Minister Yogi Adityanath, Sithraman made a remarkable statement. She said, 'The Chief Minister is doing what is the spirit behind the freedom movement.' Her comment came a month after cow vigilantes lynched Pehlu Khan in Alwar (Rajasthan), and after Sadhvi Kamal Didi praised these vigilantes and compared them to freedom fighters such as Bhagat Singh and Chandrasekhar Azad. The year before, the residents of Bisada (Uttar Pradesh) draped an Indian flag on the body of Ravin Sisodia, one of the men accused of lynching Mohammed Akhlaq and for injuring his son Danish in 2015. Then-Culture Minister Mahesh Sharma, who represented the Dadri area of Uttar Pradesh in the Lok Sabha, came and paid his respects to Sisodia, a man accused of cold-blooded murder. The glorification of the cow vigilantes goes from the village level right to the parliament and to the Union cabinet. It is not a marginal matter.

The cow vigilantes are not shy of telling their story. They do not compare themselves to freedom fighters or drape the flag over their actions. In April 2017, *India Today*'s Syed Masroor Hasan and Mohammed Hizbullah spoke to Nagendra Kumar, a spokesperson for the Rashtriya Gau Raksha Dal in Moradabad. Kumar told them – after the murder of Akhlaq – that his men are well trained. 'When we set out, we have a single objective,' Kumar said. 'We carry lathis matching our heights. If [the cattle traders] don't spare you or resist, you got to at least break their legs so that they cannot walk for the rest of their lives.' Once the gang of gau rakshaks seize a truck carrying cows, 'we inflict injuries' on the drivers and workers 'that leave no visible bruises. They should be hit hard. But there should be no bleeding'. Pushpender Sharma, the president of the Gau Rakshak Dal of Uttar Pradesh, said, 'We inflict injuries. We fracture their bones, muscles, legs. We don't hit on the head and rip it apart.' These saviours of the cow are actually highway robbers – they take the cows and distribute them amongst their activists, 'distributed there and then', said Sharma.

In July 2016, Balu Sarvaiya and some members of his family were skinning a cow in Mota Samadhiyala village in Una taluka (Gujarat). Men appeared, beat Balu and his family, took them to Una where four of the men were stripped and beaten in full view. The men being beaten were Dalits. The attackers were part of the two hundred gau rakshak groups that had sprung up in Gujarat. At that time, Gujarat's Chief Secretary G.R. Gloria told *The Hindu*'s Mahesh Langa, 'We are going to take strong action against such groups. These vigilantes are self-proclaimed gau rakshaks but in actual fact they are hooligans.' Strikingly, a senior government official – unnamed in Langa's story – said that these gau rakshaks are 'local lumpen elements who have emerged as extra-judicial forces and operate with impunity. They have become a real nuisance'. But then came the most disturbing part of the comment. This unnamed government official said that 'local policemen are complicit in the activities of these groups because they act as informers of police and also many times, they extort money from those in the animal trade or in the slaughter house line'.

The Punjab-Haryana High Court – at around this time – ordered a CBI probe into the death of Mustain, a transporter of cattle, at the hands of a Gau Raksha Dal group in Kurukshetra (Haryana) in March 2016. 'A so-called vigilante group constituted with the backing of political bosses and senior functionaries governing the state, including police', the court wrote, 'are bent upon circumventing law and fleecing poor persons ferrying their animals, be it for any personal domestic use or otherwise. . . . Apparently even the senior functionaries of the police are hand-in-glove with such vigilante groups.'

No such clarity came from the Central government. After the death of Pehlu Khan in 2017, the Union Minister Mukhtar Abbas Naqvi said, 'No such incident took place as described by the opposition. We don't condone lawlessness. No message should go that we are for cow killings.' Bizarrely, the Rajasthan police filed a First Information Report (FIR) not against the killers, but against the murdered Pehlu Khan and his sons Arif and Irfan. They were accused of being cow smugglers or those with intent to kill a cow, even as the evidence showed that they were merely cattle traders.

In the eyes of the BJP government, the mechanism of the state is there to give impunity to cow vigilantes and to terrorize ordinary people. No other explanation is possible.

IV

How do cows die in India?

The main killer is the railways. The North Central Railway noted, in August 2018, that it had seen about 1,300 cattle die on its tracks since April of that year. That was an increase of 271 per cent compared to the 2017 April-August number. In the financial year of 2015-16, Indian Railways recorded only 2,183 cases of cattle killed by trains. But, in the financial year that ended in March 2018, the number increased to 10,105 – a 362 per cent increase. These numbers are confounding. Daljit Singh, president of the Progressive Dairy Farmers' Association of Punjab, told Avishek Dastidar of *The Indian Express*, 'Cow deaths due to accidents on tracks and roads have increased, but they are mostly cows roaming astray after they stop giving milk. They are mostly desi breed. And this problem will only grow in the coming years. Is this not cow slaughter?' What Singh refers to are the cows that would – in another time – be killed for meat since they no longer produce milk. With the ban on cow slaughter, this problem of cows killed on tracks will only increase. That is why the Rail Ministry has had to 'sit up and take note'.

In 2018, Kumar Ketkar wrote, 'Surprisingly, two states, namely Madhya Pradesh and Uttar Pradesh, top the list – where people killed under the name of love of the cow are highest – as far as deaths of cows on tracks are concerned. Roughly around one third of cows killed in India on railway tracks come from these two states only.' Where, he asked, are the cow protectors?

The sudden spurt in the number of abandoned cows is directly related to the ban on cow slaughter and on the inability of the owner of the cows to feed them. The ban on cow slaughter leads to slaughter by train. Feed for the cow costs about Rs. 90 to Rs. 100 per day. This is a large expense for a farmer who cannot recover this money from milk sales. Earlier, without such stringent provisions against cattle slaughter, the farmer could – after the cow stopped producing milk – sell the cow for Rs. 5,000 to Rs. 10,000. Today, this is not possible.

The problem of stray cows drew criticism not only from the opposition but also from within the ranks of the BJP. In the Madhya Pradesh Assembly, in 2017, BJP MLA from Chandla R.K. Prajapati said that there are 20,000 stray cattle in his constituency. Chandla is not alone. It is said that 35 to 40 of Madhya Pradesh's 51 districts have been hit by stray cows. Gau Bhakts keep shouting 'cow is our mother', Prajapati says, but when he asked them, 'have you ever reared a cow', they say 'not cow, but buffalo is our mother!' 'Let there be no development in my constituency,' Prajapati said, 'but please manage the problem of stray cows.' Prajapati held his seat in the 2018 Assembly election, but the BJP lost in Madhya Pradesh. Stray cows were part of the problem.

A conservative number of stray cows for India is five million. Some of these cows die on railway tracks, others die in car accidents. But many die in cow shelters, which have been created by the cow protection movement. Delhi's cow shelters have numbers that are illustrative of the situation in India: about 20 cows die per day in the shelters from about the 17,000 that are housed in them. Cows mainly die due to starvation, dehydration and overall neglect. In Kanpur, where the shelters are considered to be well tended, about a fourth of the cows in them died in a span of five months in 2017.

Haidar Naqvi, writing in the *Hindustan Times*, pointed out that the shelter in Kanpur holds 540 cows, of which 152 had died. The cow society is not poor. It has property worth Rs. 220 crore. Baba Tiwari, who takes care of the shelter, told Naqvi that inadequate fodder had been given to the cows even as there is money in the bank and fodder in the market. A cow needs 8 kgs of hay and 15 kg of fodder a day. Caretakers told Naqvi that the cows are being given only 1 kg of hay and 2 kgs of green fodder a day. The shelter in Jaipur, considered to be the best in Asia, has seen 11,000 cow deaths in the eleven months in 2017 – three deaths every two hours.

Varun Muturkar at *Youth Ki Awaaz* exposed the rhetoric of the BJP-RSS government with regard to cow protection. He looked at five cow shelters in different parts of India and showed that the leaders are 'ready to kill and get killed for cow protection', but they look the other way when cows die in their hundreds and thousands.

1. **Jalore Gaushalas**: In July 2017, gaushalas in the district of Jalore in Rajasthan saw the death of about 700 cows due to incessant rains, worsened by a dam breaking nearby. Due

to the rains, the cows could not get up and they needed to be lifted and then tended. Due to a lack of proper fodder, swept away by flood, many cows died of starvation and weakness. Apart from the death of about 700 cows, 3,300 more cows and calves were injured. Pathmeda Trust, which runs a number of gaushalas in the state, alleged that the government didn't help. Ironically, the state is ruled by the BJP and has a department dedicated to cow welfare.

2. **Hingonia Gaushala**: The Jalore deaths could be the result of inadequate response to a natural phenomenon, but in the year before these deaths, Rajasthan saw worse. Over 500 cows died in just 10 days in August at the Hingonia gaushala in Jaipur, where about a 1,000 die in a month on average. For a shelter claimed to be the 'best' in Asia, the cow-death statistics were pretty bad for the year. The state government said 8,122 cows had died between just January and July in 2016. The death rate had increased from 7.09 per cent in 2012 (INC government) to 11.31 per cent in July 2016 (BJP government), according to statistics released by the state government.

   The deaths at the shelter appear to be more systemic. '*There is acute shortage of green fodder, mineral and vitamins that can help the diseased cow recover. Here only dry fodder is provided that just helps them sustain*', a source at the shelter had told *Times of India* in 2015. Moreover, according to the statistics released by Hingonia Gaushala, about 90 cows die every day in Jaipur inside and outside the gaushala. Around 40 died daily on average at the then Jaipur Municipal Corporation-run gaushala. Not much far from Hingonia, Pehlu Khan was lynched in Alwar by some self-proclaimed gau rakshaks in 2017, who accused him of smuggling cows.

3. **Shagun Gaushala**: The Shagun Gaushala in Durg of Chhattisgarh, another BJP-ruled state, saw the death of about 200 cows in a week last year in the month of August. The gaushala was owned by a local BJP leader Harish Verma who was then also the BJP vice president of Jamulnagar panchayat. According to a report by *The Indian Express*, similar conditions were prevalent at two other gaushalas run by Verma nearby. The cows died because of a lack of care. State veterinary department officials said the deaths at the shelter were due to a lack of fodder and water.

   If this appears to be a case of one bad politician, it wasn't so. In November 2014, the Chhattisgarh Lok Aayog had flagged 27 gaushalas as errant, including the Shagun Gaushala, alleging they mismanaged government funds. Despite that, from 2015-16 onward, nearly 30 per cent of funds disbursed by the Chhattisgarh Gau Seva Aayog went to 25 of these gaushalas.

4. **Kanpur Gaushala**: About 28 per cent of cows at a gaushala said to be the country's richest died within 5 months last year, under the watch of the Yogi Adityanath government. Yogi Adityanath is known for tending cows even in his home in Gorakhpur, but perhaps he and his deputy chief ministers were too busy to get the funds given to Kanpur Gaushala investigated. The cow deaths were basically due to improper fodder fed to cows. Perhaps it is another Chaara Ghotala. Union Minister Maneka Gandhi is the patron of a gaushala in Pilibhit district. According to an *India Today* report this shelter and one in Shahjahanpur are also affected by lack of fodder and space. '*Earlier, we used to sell healthy cows and bulls to the farmers, the money was used to run the shelter, but with the new BJP government in place, farmers are scared to come*

here,' caretaker of the Pilibhit shelter told *India Today*.

5. **Gaushalas in Haryana**: Manohar Lal Khattar, the BJP chief minister of Haryana, has said in the past that Muslims can live in India but shouldn't eat beef. He too doesn't seem to be too keen on protecting cows otherwise though. A report of *India TV* shows that about 2,000 cows are suffering in a government-run gaushala, all because the gaushalas turned into a wetland. In another gaushala named Shri Krishna Gaushala in Kurukshetra, about 25 cows lost their lives due to mismanagement.

A quantum jump in deaths of cows coming under speeding trains, and deaths of hundreds cows due to starvation or unhealthy upkeep at cow shelters, are not the only cause of their mass deaths.

Perhaps the biggest killer of cows could be said to be plastic, especially its most common variety polyethylene. In June 2017, *The Times of India* reported that 1,000 cows die each year in Lucknow because they eat plastics. In most of these deaths, the animal dies due to multiple organ failure and about 50-55 kgs of polythene is found in the stomach of the dead cow. The cow dies a very painful death. The plastics impact the cow's immune system and – if medical attention is not immediately provided – 'the hind legs of the cows get paralysed, functioning in rumen slows [sic] and blood circulation is affected due to toxins present in the polythene', says the senior veterinary officer at Kanha Upvan, Jay Prakash. Chief veterinary officer of Lucknow, Tej Singh Yadav, told *The Times of India*, that 'clusters of polythene are taken out in rock solid state from their rumens', namely the stomach. This is in Lucknow.

Across India, say activists Clementien Pauws and Rukmini Sekhar, plastic is the great killer of cows. Rukmini – who is an animal rights activist – and Clementien Pauws – who runs a society for the welfare of cows – have filed a petition in the Supreme Court to ban plastic bags because they severely impact the lives of animals. Their 34-minute documentary – *Plastic Cow* – available on YouTube – suggests that to save the cow two things need to be done: ban use of plastic for garbage disposal and stop open dumping of daily waste.

In the mid-1990s, the Chief Minister of Delhi – Sahib Singh Verma of the BJP – said, 'Consumption of plastic is a major killer of cows in the capital of the country.' No idea what the RSS and its cow protectors said about this fact or what they believe now. Easier for them to blame minorities than to deal with the real facts of the matter. India, according to the Central Pollution Control Board, generates 15,342 tonnes of plastic waste a day – of which 9,205 tonnes are reportedly recycled. That leaves 6,137 tonnes – or 40 per cent – to fly around the streets. It is what the cows eat and it is how the cows die.

In March 2016, the Central government laid out its Plastic Waste Management Rules. They were amended, or should we say diluted, in April 2018. This was just two months before India hosted the World Environment Day with the theme 'Beat Plastic Pollution'. Vendors who gave out plastic carry bags had to register and pay a minimum fee of Rs. 48,000 per year. This was now amended away. The government gave away an important tool to reduce plastic waste. The plastic industry, of course, is aiding the government's lackadaisical attitude.

The Rules from 2016 would have phased out 'non-recyclable multi-layered plastic' in two years. On 27 March 2018, the amendment said that the government would get rid of only 'multi-layered plastic which is non-recyclable or non-energy recoverable with no alternate use'. This provided an escape route, since the packaging material – if not directly recycled – could be put to some other use. Plastic makers used this loophole to continue using this material. So there it is.

It is worth recording that in Una, where the attack on Dalits was severe and the resistance fierce, Dalit activists went to the Collector's office in Surendranagar to tell the government and the cow lovers that 'more cows die due to lack of fodder, water and plastics than at the hand of the slaughter houses'. This was ignored.

In 2015, an exhibition was held in Jaipur called *Bovine Divine*. The artist Siddhartha Kararwal created a four-pound cow made of Styrofoam and then let it be suspended in the air by a large balloon. The point of the exhibit, said Kararwal, was to raise awareness about the perils before cows by plastic bags in the streets. The police came and said that the exhibit had to be removed because it hurt the sensibilities of people. A mysterious organization arrived at Jawahar Kala Kendra, where the exhibition was being held, and took possession of the cow. Vida Sagar, an organizer of the exhibit, said that these unidentified people then 'worshipped the cow and garlanded it'. This was the Styrofoam cow.

V

When Narendra Modi led the charge for the 2014 elections, he told a gathering in Bihar in April, 'This country wants a Green Revolution but those at the Centre want a Pink Revolution.' The phrase was strange. What is a Pink Revolution? 'When animals are slaughtered,' Modi explained, 'the colour of their flesh is pink.' He suggested that the government was subsidising slaughterhouses and was interested in the profits from meat exports. The government in Delhi, he said, 'is not willing to provide subsidy to a person who keeps a cow, but if a person wants to set up a slaughterhouse, he gets assistance'. Elsewhere, Modi wrote, 'it saddens me that the present government led by the Congress is promoting slaughtering cows and exporting beef to bring a Pink Revolution'.

Modi's ally Maneka Gandhi said that the profits from illegal slaughter and from the export of animals funded terrorist organizations.

All this is as it is. Once the BJP government took power, however, the meat exports began to *increase*. Between the months of April and November 2014, India exported meat to the tune of $3.3 billion. This was with the BJP in power. In the previous year, when the BJP was not in power, the meat sales were only $2.8 billion. Since the export of cow meat is banned in India, the meat exported was largely (97 per cent) buffalo meat. No BJP leader would comment on this increase. The Congress leader Manish Tewari, on the other hand, said, 'While in Opposition the Prime Minister is at the forefront of slamming the purported pink revolution and when in government he is at the forefront of promoting it as evidenced by the rise in export figures.'

India is the third largest exporter of beef in the world, according to the figures provided by the Food and Agriculture Organization (FAO) and the Organization for Economic Cooperation (OECD). It follows Brazil and Australia. To maintain this position, the BJP government continues to offer grants of up to Rs. 15 crore to set up new slaughterhouses or to modernize old ones. The total amount spent on this subsidy from 2014 to 2017 has been Rs. 68 crore. Most subsidies when to states with a BJP government.

VI

In 1966, the BJP leader K.R. Malkani said that the flesh of the cow which died a natural death can be eaten. There was a rapid slide from Malkani's views to the current state of affairs. But have things really changed or is hypocrisy the mode?

In 2015, the RSS leader Manmohan Vaidya went to Arunachal Pradesh. At a press conference in Itanagar, the prachar pramukh of the RSS went on about beef. People in Arunachal Pradesh, he said, consume beef. 'We don't tell society what to eat or not to eat,' Vaidya said. People who eat beef, he pointed out, can join the RSS. The RSS in Arunachal Pradesh had about 3,000 members, many of whom ate beef.

This was a curious press conference. For a movement that pushed for cow protection to now say that it was not telling people what to eat – remarkable. But Vaidya was not far from the second supremo of the RSS, Golwalkar, who told a Vishwa Hindu Parishad conference in Guwahati (Assam) in 1967 that Adivasis, who make up a large part of the population, do eat beef even as they are Hindus. Their geographic distance from the Hindu heartland, he said, and economic necessity took them to beef eating. Golwalkar did not insist that they give up beef.

In many of the states of the North-East – such as Meghalaya, Mizoram and Nagaland – which are Christian majority, the RSS has been flexible on the issue of beef consumption. If the BJP had taken up the beef issue in the North-East as it had in the Gangetic plains, it would not have been able to hold power in Arunachal Pradesh, Assam, Manipur and Tripura and it would not be able to form an alliance in Meghalaya and Nagaland. 'No cow slaughter ban would be enforced in the North-eastern states,' said the BJP as it went to the polls, allowing Asaduddin Owaisi of the All-India Majlis-e-Ittehadul Muslimeen to say, 'BJP's hypocrisy is that in Uttar Pradesh cow is mummy, but in the North-east cow is yummy.'

VII

In 2017, Vikas Rawal, a professor of economics at Jawaharlal Nehru University, underlined the challenge faced by India as a result of cow protection laws. The number of unproductive cattle has gone up, he wrote in a study entitled 'On Economic Implications of the Restrictions on Cow Slaughter'. The number now is 27 crore unproductive cattle in India. It would cost Rs. 5.40 lakh crore per year to look after these cows. That figure is five times the defence budget of India. It would require five lakh acres of land to house this cattle. They would consume more water than is consumed by all Indians. The implications of the increase in unproductive cattle are startling. Rawal says that India has one third of the world's stunted children. This stunting is attributed to low protein intake. If these children ate more animal products, they would be healthier. This includes milk. Milk production will decline as a consequence of the lack of incentive for farmers to rear cattle. India might have to import milk as a consequence. This will have a catastrophic impact on an already fragile agrarian system.

There are political benefits to the RSS-BJP from the cow vigilantes and from the cow protection movement. But the implications are terrible for India, terrible for those killed and terrible for the economy. But these people do not care. They are happy to launch an ambulance service for cows, when there are no such services for humans in those areas. More money will be spent to take care of cows than to take care of humans.

In Bulandshahar (Uttar Pradesh), a cow mob lynched a police officer called Subodh Kumar Singh as well as another man. The cow fanatics were led by Yogesh Raj of the Bajrang Dal. He vanished. The government of Yogi Adityanath first showed remorse for the cow carcasses found in a field – whose deaths were not yet investigated. There was no word on the lynching of a policeman and of the other man. It was only after protests, that the government made a few remarks about the deaths of the humans. This is not new. In October 2002, a lynch mob killed five Dalits in front of a police station in Dulina, Jhajjar (Haryana). The police sent the dead cows for examination and booked the dead Dalits for cow slaughter. Giriraj Kishore of the Vishwa Hindu Parishad offered what is the standard RSS-BJP logic, 'Cow is considered more sacred than human beings in the *Puranas*.'

FOUR. *SILENCING CASTE, SANITIZING OPPRESSION*

> The Hindu Social Order is based upon a division of labour which reserves for the Hindus clean and respectable jobs and assigns to the untouchables dirty and mean jobs and thereby clothes the Hindus with dignity and heaps ignominy upon the untouchables.
>
> – Dr. B.R. Ambedkar

'Cows are more sacred than human beings,' said Giriraj Kishore of the Vishwa Hindu Parishad. What Kishore said here is not unique. It is normal in the ranks of the RSS and the BJP, particularly when it comes to caste and Dalits. The old RSS leadership wanted the *Manusmriti* to be the Indian Constitution. They wanted caste hierarchy to be sacrosanct. Seventy years later, the RSS-BJP view remains medieval, particularly when it comes to caste hierarchy. The RSS-BJP has struggled here – wanting to unite all Hindus on the one hand, while refusing to challenge the system of graded hierarchy – or caste – on the other. But it has sought to tackle the contradiction in several clichéd ways.

First, it falsely blames the legacy of caste on the Mughals and the British. Second, it peddles the view that the religious minorities – mainly Muslims – are a threat and so Hindu unity needs to be built. Third, it pretends to tackle the basis of caste hierarchy without doing anything to undermine caste hierarchy.

The most recent attempt to pretend to tackle caste came in

the way of the Swachh Bharat Abhiyan or Clean India Mission launched by the Modi government in October 2014. The Mission came with five objectives:

1. Eradicate manual scavenging.
2. Eliminate open defecation by the construction of toilets for households and communities.
3. Introduce modern and scientific solid waste management practices.
4. Enable private sector participation in the sanitation.
5. Change people's attitudes towards sanitation and create awareness.

By themselves, these goals are very good. In the context of the BJP policy, they are a smokescreen.

I

The BJP government is not the first to take up the issue of sanitation. The previous government had a Clean India scheme – the Nirmal Bharat Abhiyan, which was earlier known as the Total Sanitation Campaign. But this time, with the BJP programme, the propaganda machinery of the government – with all the help of the media – promoted the 'novelty' of the scheme and its 'innovativeness'.

Sanjay, a ragpicker in Mehrauli, told Mallica Joshi of the *Hindustan Times*, in October 2014 that he was bewildered by the scene of ministers and bureaucrats going about cleaning the streets. 'These are the same people from whose houses we pick up garbage every day,' he said. 'This is part of our life. We don't really understand why they are making it such a big deal.' Sanjay is part of a large group of sanitation workers and ragpickers, largely invisible, who manage the garbage of Delhi's 20 million people. Without them, the city would come to a halt. People like Sanjay have no part in the Clean India campaign. Sanjay was removed from the scene. Mahatma Gandhi appeared, only as the patron saint of cleanliness, not as the fighter against colonialism and fanaticism. This is typical of the saffron fanatics, to take Gandhi but leave his politics behind.

The BJP approach to sanitation is deeply rooted in a very conservative nationalist and caste-ridden worldview. The idea was to project a *samras* or harmonious picture of Indian society, where cleanliness is connected to one's *kartavya* or duty towards Bharat Mata or Mother India. Modi's oath towards a clean India suggests this view – '*Ab hamara kartavya hai ki gandagi ko door karke Bharat Mata ki sewa karein* (Now, it is our duty to serve Mother India by removing the dirt)'. These are simple, obvious slogans. But the context of such slogans are important, for beneath them and around them lie much more difficult realities. The idea of duty, for instance, sneaks in the caste hierarchy and ideas of caste duty. Old historical asymmetries and injustices make their way to the centre of these discussions.

Without a conversation about caste and cleanliness, the idea of Clean India would merely reproduce old hierarchies in a caste-ridden society. A population is already condemned – along the lines of caste – to clean and to remove garbage. They are stigmatized. A technical solution to a social problem might be helpful, but it might also – as in this case – merely retain the hierarchies. Reforming individuals or providing new technologies will not shake the roots of the caste system, the reason why cleanliness is such a fraught issue in India. The deliberate sociological blindness towards caste has led to certain outcomes. What we see with the Clean India campaign is not a more clean India, but a hardening of the hierarchy of caste.

II

Photo-journalist Sudharak Olwe has an important photo essay called 'In Search of Dignity and Justice'. It gives us a window into the lives of cleaners – sweepers and ragpickers. There are an enormous number of workers who are employed to clean our society. In the Greater Mumbai Municipal Corporation there are 30,000 conservancy workers. Olwe writes,

> All of them are dalits, belonging to the lowest rung of the caste system. They have little or no education. Without exception, all of them despise their work. They are completely ignored or looked down upon with disgust by the rest of the society. They have to work in the midst of filth, with no protective gear, not even access to water to wash off the slime. Most of them are alcoholics.

The point about alcohol needs a caveat. The jobs are often so filthy that it would be remarkable if the workers did not turn to something like alcohol to numb the smell and the filth. It is impossible, workers say, to 'enter the sea of filth' without being dulled. Olwe goes into this kind of detail because he wants 'citizens to see the workers and to acknowledge their presence and contribution'. The pictures in the exhibition do not sooth the eye. The country, Olwe writes, needs to acknowledge the contribution the workers 'make for our health and survival, at the cost of their own health and survival'. One has to remain patient and not merely look at the pictures but look beyond them – reminding ourselves of the stark fact that millions and millions of people in this country, equal citizens of this republic, are condemned to live subhuman lives so that the rest of society can look 'clean'. The workers are invisible, always invisible.

Olwe's project reminds me of my own blood-curdling experience in 2004 with the death of workers in sewers. A newspaper reported on these deaths. A group of us talked to officials in the Safai Karamchari Commission, we met a few families who had lost their young sons in the sewers and we collected information about the working conditions of workers in the sewers. We began a campaign to make it clear that in Delhi alone about a hundred workers die each year in the sewers, a silent genocide of workers that is a blot on our democracy. We distributed handbills, staged a street play, held corner meetings and held a big public meeting at the Constitution Club (Delhi).

The handbill we created was titled 'City Sewers or Deathtraps?' It starts with details of deaths of two workers – Ala and Umesh – on 12 June 2004 while they were cleaning the sewer at Samaypur Badli, then moves on to the 'powers that be who never appear to be unduly disturbed with such deaths' and also questions the media which is 'always on the prowl for sensational news' but remains silent over such deaths. It also mentions why none of the Safai Karmacharis are even provided elementary instruments such as rope, box, oxygen cylinder, and masks at the time of descending down into the gutters. It ends with a few questions about sewer workers not getting adequate compensation in case of death or injury, nobody getting prosecuted for such deaths or calling such deaths 'murders'.

Believe me, when I was re-reading the handbill, I felt that we were really naive as far as the issue was concerned. Naive about the gravity of the situation as it exists and also about the remedies which were and still are offered to ameliorate it.

Three years later, S. Anand did a story called 'Life Inside a Black Hole' for *Tehelka*. He wrote, 'Beneath the glitter of India are dark alleys in which are trapped poisonous gases and millions of Dalits who do our dirty job in return for disease and untouchability.' The data in the text is mind-numbing. Anand writes,

> At least 22,327 Dalits of a sub-community die doing sanitation work every year. Safai Kamgar Vikas Sangh, a body representing sanitation workers of the Brihanmumbai Municipal Corporation (BMC), sought data under the Right to Information Act in 2006, and found that 288 workers had died in 2004-05, 316 in 2003-04, and 320 in 2002-03, in just 14 of the 24 wards of the BMC. About 25 deaths every month. These figures do not include civic hospital workers, gutter cleaners or sanitation workers on contract. Compare this with the 5,100 soldiers – army, police, paramilitaries – who have died between 1990 and 2007 combating militancy in Jammu & Kashmir.

The report underlined the fact that these are not the only deaths which can be attributed to exposure to poisonous gases. Most of the workers who work in sewers die before retirement. The average lifespan of a manhole worker is about 45 years. And as expected, if a worker does not die inside a manhole, then there is no monetary compensation. Such deaths are considered a logical fallout of occupational hazard for which the workers get a 'risk allowance', which is Rs. 50 in Delhi.

The report quotes Ashish Mittal, an occupational health physician who had done a study on sewer workers, who raises the situation of sewage workers in other countries. Manhole workers in these other countries, Mittal says, 'are protected in bunny suits to avoid contact with contaminated water and sport a respiratory apparatus; the sewers are well-lit, mechanically aerated with huge fans and therefore are not so oxygen deficient. In Hong Kong, a sewer worker, after adequate training, needs at least 15 licences and permits to enter a manhole'. India is in a different situation:

> The manhole worker wears nothing more than a loincloth or half-pants. In Delhi, since the directives of the National Human Rights Commission in October 2002, the majority of the DJB's permanent

> workers wear a 'safety belt'. It's a joke. This belt, connecting the worker through thick ropes to men standing outside, offers no protection from the gases and the sharp objects that assault the worker. At best, it helps haul them out when they faint or die.

The concluding part of the report emphasized that it is not the lack of funds or technology which poses problems. If technology could be used to launch satellites then why can it not be used for garbage and sewage? Detailing the allotment of thousands of crores of rupees for drainage and sewerage work, it posed a question: why does so much money get spent on laying and relaying pipes and drains that are designed to kill? 'India's urban planners, designers and technologists have never felt the need to conceive a human-friendly system of managing garbage and sewage. Instead, they rely on an unending source of disposable, cheap, Dalit labour,' he writes.

Perhaps the hiatus which separates the 'almost invisible sewer worker' mostly belonging to the Dalit caste and the articulate sections of our society and their complete detachment from the pain and agony they face could be described by a Radio Mirchi television commercial which found mention in the same write-up and the reaction (or rather its absence) which it generated. That commercial was on air for close to two years. It began with a song that emerged out of a manhole – *Yeh suhana mausam, yeh khula aasmaan, kho gaye hum yahaan, haye, kho gaye hum yahaan* . . . (This lovely weather, these wide open skies, we are lost in the bliss, oh, we are lost here . . .). Viewers could see a paan-chewing man in a safari suit wondering what keeps the man down in the manhole so happy that he should sing. Zooming in on the trousers and footwear left beside the manhole cover, the tagline said, *Mirchi Sunnewaale . . . Always Khush*. Conceived by Prasoon Joshi of McCann Erickson, the ad went on without a murmur of protest from viewers or civil rights groups.

III

Twenty-two thousand workers die each year just to keep the sewers unclogged, and many more die before they reach retirement age. To this comes an advertisement that shows the sewage worker singing happily.

But then comes Divya Bharathi's *Kakkoos* (The Toilet), a film from 2017. The film targets the tradition that people from a particular community must clean human waste. It is a scathing critique of society and of the Swachh Bharat campaign. The film is dedicated to 'your conspiracy of silence on the septic tank deaths'. It should have gone further – it should have been dedicated to 'your connivance as well'. The film was so sharp that many cases were lodged against it and the police prevented its screening. The police raided Bharathi's house more than once just for making a film on manual scavenging.

Caste and such discriminations are so common and ingrained in our psyche that nobody finds them to be abominable. The profession of cleaning – the hierarchy that sets these professions into stone – has become part of the common sense of Indian culture. India's ruling class yearns to make India an economic superpower, yet does nothing to change the conditions that make half of our population defecate in the open, and that maintain a profession of shit collection that employs lakhs of people. These communities – whether Valmikis or Thottis – share the same fate: they are oppressed by a caste hierarchy that forces them into the least desirable occupations, which in a collapsed job market, becomes their tragic fate, with caste and capitalism conspiring to hold them down.

Modi launched the Clean India Mission in October 2014 from the same Valmiki *basti* where Gandhi had stayed in the 1940s. It was not important to Modi that to do so, eight decades later, would further stigmatize the community, cement the association of 'cleaner' with the Valmikis. Modi has a view of caste that is deeply reactionary. In his book *Karmyog*, he calls cleaning a 'spiritual experience', a view that derives from the most deeply cynical approach to the real world experience of sewage work. Modi's book was a collection of speeches to IAS officials. It was published by the Gujarat government. The Gujarat State Petroleum Corporation, a top ranking public sector unit, was roped in to fund 5,000 copies of the book. Here is Modi talking about Safai Kamdars or sanitation workers:

> I do not believe that they have been doing this job just to sustain their livelihood. Had this been so, they would not have continued with this type of job generation after generation. . . . At some point of time, somebody must have got the enlightenment that it is their (Valmikis') duty to work for the happiness of the entire society and the Gods; that they have to do this job bestowed upon them by Gods; and that this job of cleaning up should continue as an internal spiritual activity for centuries. This should have continued generation after generation. It is impossible to believe that their ancestors did not have the choice of adopting any other work or business.

Bezwada Wilson is a leader in the Safai Karamchari Andolan. He offers a different view of sanitation work. In the foreword to *India Stinking*, Wilson writes,

> How can one feel proud of cleaning the worm filled, stench producing shits of millions every day? Instinctively closing our nostrils, filling our chests with what fresh air we can muster before entering these toilets, we safai karamcharis suffer from the worst kinds of respiratory and skin infections. . . . [M]any would tell us how at the age of eight or eleven they were introduced to this work; how for many days

> they could not bring food to their lips; how the stench of shit was constantly in their nostrils; how they were constantly spitting out the shame and the indignity.

Modi's *Karmyog* is in line with the general view of sanitation work by the committees set up in independent India – such as the Barve Committee (1949) and the Malkani Committee (1965). The Barve Committee suggested that sanitation workers did not consider their work to be dirty:

> Ancestors of these Bhangis were just field labourers of a low caste, but never did the work of scavenging. Some of these people took to the dirty work of cleansing the latrines for the sake of profit. Slowly this developed into a monopoly. The stage was reached when the Bhangis wanted to exploit this monopoly and a sort of customary right was thus developed. By force of habit the Bhangi lost his self-respect to such an extent that he did not consider the dirty work of cleansing latrines as a curse from which he should endeavour to extricate himself.

The Malkani Committee focused on the 'customary' work of the sanitation workers. 'Scavenging has been a way of life for the family,' it noted. 'A fatalistic attitude pervades the whole outlook due to the lack of education and the absence of other openings for employment.' Modi is in line with these conservative reports that condemn the sanitation worker to this horrible – and anachronistic – job.

When Modi's remarks about 'spiritual experience' were published in a few Tamil newspapers, there was a massive reaction from Dalits and others in the state. Effigies of Modi were burnt. Modi withdrew copies of his book, but remained with his opinion. Two years later, in 2009, Modi addressed 9,000 safai karamcharis.

He said that their job was like that of a temple priest. 'A priest cleans a temple every day before prayers, you also clean the city like a temple. You and the temple priest work alike.' Gandhi had similarly praised 'scavenging as the noblest service to society' (*Navajivan*, 8 January 1925). Dr. B.R. Ambedkar was sharp. He called such patronizing ideas 'the doom of the Untouchable'. Clean India with sanitation workers in the current conditions is the opposite of a clean India. It dooms Dalits. It does not liberate them.

IV

In 2016, *The Hindu* reported on a curious matter at Chennai airport. Manual scavenging is banned in India and in Tamil Nadu. Yet it continues, with 99 per cent of these workers from Dalit communities and amongst them 95 per cent are women. Chennai airport was modernized at a cost of Rs. 2,000 crore. And yet, the paper said that it had spoken to sources who said that workers cleaned manholes on the airport premises without any protective gear. Four people, including three sanitation workers, had been asphyxiated while cleaning a septic tank in Okkiyum Thoraipakkam. Over the past two decades, *The Hindu* noted, about two hundred workers had died in Tamil Nadu while cleaning the sewers and septic tanks. This job, it needs to be said again, is already illegal and yet, on government property, it takes place routinely.

Chennai is not alone. Delhi is in as poor shape. Darpan Singh, writing in *India Today*, says that the situation in Delhi is 'very bad'. In 2015, the Delhi High Court had rebuked the municipal government and asked them to complete a survey on the number of sanitation workers – notably manual scavengers – in the city. India banned manual scavenging in 1993, but in 2013 the parliament passed a new law that would punish anyone with a five year prison term if they hired people to clean toilets. It shows how weak the enforcement of the ban has been. In 2015, the government's Census data showed that there are lakhs of manual scavengers across the country – despite the ban and the new law. Maharashtra leads the way, with Uttar Pradesh just behind.

The government figures for those involved in manual scavenging (just under 2 lakhs) is an undercount. Others say that the actual figure is near 13 lakhs.

Why does this practice continue? The Planning Commission – before it was shut down by Modi's government – suggested that this was due to a 'lack of water-serviced latrines'. But this does not seem an adequate answer. All parliamentary measures to end manual scavenging have been half-hearted. The Barve Committee (1949) for Maharashtra and the Malkani Committee (1965) for India came up with tepid recommendations. The government laws to ban manual scavenging have been weak. The Employment of Manual Scavengers and Construction of Dry Latrines (Prohibition) Act came in 1993 – decades after Independence – and even this was not notified in the Gazette of India till 1997. No state bothered to promulgate the act till 2000. There has been no conviction of any government official or any firm in the past twenty years. The main violators are government agencies – such as the Indian Railways – but they are not made to comply with the law nor are they punished when they violate the law.

As if to acknowledge the failure of this Act the government passed new legislation in September 2013 called The Prohibition of Employment as Manual Scavengers and their Rehabilitation Act. The Act provides an escape clause for local and railway authorities, who have made the argument that they cannot afford to get rid of manual scavenging. The laws seek to provide workers with protective gear and other safety precautions rather than to substitute humans with machines (which are widely available). If this protective gear is used, the Act stipulates, the workers are no longer 'manual scavengers'.

In 2014, Human Rights Watch published a report – *Cleaning Human Waste* – which assessed these two new laws that have come out in the past two and a half decades. The organization makes some important recommendations for the Indian government and for the governments of the Indian states:

1. Identify all individuals currently engaged in manual scavenging.
2. Ensure that rehabilitation entitlements under the 2013 Act are available to manual scavenging communities.
3. Take immediate steps to ensure that officials effectively intervene to stop communities from being coerced to practise manual scavenging.
4. Strictly enforce the law against local government officials who themselves employ people to work as manual scavengers.
5. Enact The Scheduled Castes and Scheduled Tribes (Prevention of Atrocities) Amendment Ordinance, 2014, No. 1 of 2014.

The report shows that women are often compelled to continue this work not for wages but for food and community resources.

The International Labour Organization's *Resource Handbook to End Manual Scavenging* throws additional light on the persistence of this practice. It suggests that the practice continues for the following four reasons:

1. Endurance of cultural notions of caste pollution and purity and assignment of persons to the despised work based on their birth.

2. Caste inequalities layered with gender discrimination (as most dry toilet cleaners are women).
3. Apathy and failure of the state administrations throughout India to implement the law banning manual scavenging and implementation of official rehabilitation schemes.
4. Culture of impunity and the absence of state accountability, answerability and public sincerity to end caste discrimination resulting in its continuance.

Swachh Bharat does not tackle these issues. It evades them. The government, since 2014, has cut the budgetary allocation for the rehabilitation of manual scavengers by over 95 per cent. In 2014-15, the budget allowance for Self-Employment for the Rehabilitation of Manual Scavengers was Rs. 448 crore. By 2017-18, that number was reduced to just Rs. 5 crore, after being a mere Rs. 10 crore in 2016-17. There is no interest in the rehabilitation of the sanitation workers. The budget shows this. It also shows that in this time the government spent Rs. 530 crore to promote the Swachh Bharat or Clean India Mission in the media. More money was spent to *promote* the media blitz for Clean India than was spent at its highest point for the rehabilitation of the sanitation workers. These are the values of the Modi government, laid out in rupees.

V

Half of India's population defecates in the open. This was confirmed by the 2011 socio-economic Census. Open defecation means that someone has to clean up the mess. This person is often a 'manual scavenger' or a sanitation worker who collects excreta from open spaces. A United Nations study in 2014 shows that about 597 million Indians defecate in the open. That's about 61 per cent of the total number of people who defecate in the open around the world. The country that is nearest to India is Indonesia, with 54 million and then Pakistan with 41 million. China, which has a population comparable to India, only has 10 million people who defecate in the open. The number of people in India who defecate in the open has increased from 2006 (55 per cent) to 2013 (61 per cent). This was a period when India had a high growth rate. It did not convert into ending this practice, which is a danger to health and to dignity.

A report by the World Health Organization and UNICEF in 2015 showed that open defecation in India has decreased since 1990, but that the rate of decrease is very slow – notably 2 per cent per year from 1990 to 2015. In this same period, Bangladesh nearly eliminated its open defecation from 34 per cent to 1 per cent.

India has launched satellites into space, has even shot them out of the sky. India has nuclear weapons and a major army. Yet, India – which is the world's largest importer of weapons – has been unable to deal with open defecation. Development specialists often suggest that this has to do with poverty (although those weapons are somehow easily purchased).

Data from the WHO, UNICEF, the World Bank and the Government of India, however, suggests that poverty is not a sufficient explanation. There is no relation between a country's per capita GDP and the prevalence of open defecation. Three African countries, the Democratic Republic of the Congo, Malawi and Burundi, have a per capita GDP (as per purchasing power parity) of 439, 739 and 737 respectively. The open defecation rate in these countries is merely 9, 7 and 3 per cent. India, with a per capita GDP of 5,050 has an open defecation rate of 48 percent. Three of India's neighbours – Afghanistan (per capita GDP of 1,892; open defecation rate of 15 per cent), Bangladesh (per capita GDP of 2,364; open defecation rate of 3 per cent) and Pakistan (per capita GDP of 4,360; open defecation rate of 23 per cent) – are in much better shape than India. The data from these international agencies shows that India has very low rates of improvement. This is alarming and revealing.

Sangita Vyas – a research fellow at Rice University – travelled to 3,500 rural households in six states in northern India in 2014. She found that sanitation is 'just not a priority among many rural households'. Most Indians she interacted with did not think that using a toilet is good for their health. Half believe that defecating in the open is better for health than going to a latrine. People she spoke with had an 'expensive idea of what constitutes a toilet'. For many people in rural India, she writes, a toilet 'is either a large cement septic tank with a cement superstructure, or a field'. Government latrines are not seen as latrines. They are left unused.

Why are large septic tanks and expensive toilets the only thing that dominant castes will use? Because, Vyas finds – in a 2015 paper she co-authored – 'although some conservative rural Hindus find latrines of any sort distasteful, most people feel that expensive latrines with large pits or septic tanks are not polluting'. The idea of 'pollution' is key. It means that caste hierarchy and caste prejudice – not the lack of water-flush latrines – are at the heart of India's problems.

The point about pollution is further developed by Gita Ramaswamy, in *India Stinking*, who writes,

> In large parts of western world, the connection between human excreta and disease is well established. Human excreta is the principal vehicle for the transmission and spread of a wide range of communicable diseases. . . . In India, excreta is seen as impure. . . . Traditional practice has failed to keep up with scientific disposal of excreta, leading to skewed practices, particularly in the matter of having someone else to clean up behind us. Excreta avoidance

> is ritualized: the bath is taken after defecation. . . . Caste Hindu society did not ever mind that public places were soiled by excreta but insisted that inside of the house should be free of excretions. . . . Given such ritual avoidance of excreta, and the reality that excreta cannot be avoided after all, caste Hindu society, not surprisingly, found the solution in 'polluted' castes who would manually handle excreta. Scavenging and caste are thus intimately linked.

Hindu notions of purity and pollution are linked with the caste system and the practice of untouchability – and these produce the conditions for unsanitary India. Manual scavenging and open defecation are a consequence of caste hierarchy rather than of poverty and an absence of technology. This is not admitted by the BJP government, by the dominant castes and by the Indian establishment.

It is important to point out that the focus needs to be on the caste system practised by the dominant Hindu castes. Mihir Sharma's *Restart: The Last Chance for the Indian Economy* (2014) notes that 80 per cent of Hindus who live in rural areas defecate in the open fields, while only half of the Muslims do so. Near 40 per cent of Hindus who have access to a working government latrine 'won't use it', Sharma writes, whereas only 7 per cent of Muslims will defecate outside if given a choice. Sharma's data is affirmed by a paper written by two economists from the University of Texas, Michael Geruso and Dean Spears (*Sanitation and Health Externalities: Resolving the Muslim Morality Paradox*, 2014). Geruso and Spears show that the prevalence of 'open defecation is particularly high among India's Hindu majority', with about 67 per cent of Hindu households defecating in the open. In comparison, they find that 'only 42 per cent of the relatively poorer Muslim households do so'. They cite Gita Ramaswamy's *India Stinking* and Ravichandran Bathran's paper from *Economic & Political*

Weekly ('Indian Sanitation', 2011) to show that persistence of open defecation amongst Hindus is due to the 'persistence of the Hindu caste system: the ritual avoidance of excreta is maintained not only by keeping defecation away from the home, but also by relegating its clean-up to the untouchable'.

Why does open defecation persist? Because of the caste system, and because of the availability of cheap Dalit labour to do these dehumanizing jobs. Policymakers avoid this obvious explanation.

VI

Policymakers, including the Modi government, believe that building toilets is the answer to open defecation. There was once a plan to build seven toilets every minute, but now the aspiration is to build thirty toilets per minute or one toilet every two seconds.

But are toilets used? A National Sample Survey Organisation assessment from 2012 suggests that rural toilets are unused. In 2015, a Comptroller and Auditor General of India (CAG) report suggested that 'more than 30 per cent of individual household latrines were defunct/non-functional for reasons of poor quality of construction, incomplete structure, non-maintenance'.

Are toilets built holistically? Toilets might be built, but there is no thought about the sanitation chain and access to water. The sanitation chain includes the toilet (where the excreta is collected), the removal and transport of faecal sludge, subsequent treatment and final safe disposal. If the excreta is not properly disposed, then the sanitation chain remains incomplete and the sewage can contaminate land as well as water leading to health problems of different kinds.

Are toilets built so as to liberate Dalits? The answer is no, with the most hideous evidence coming from government schools in Jaipur (Rajasthan). Radha Shekhawat asked the Rajasthan High

Court to authorize the Bharat Bal Vigyan Samiti to survey schools in Jaipur. The Report, filed in 2015, showed that of the 138 schools 24 schools have no toilets for girls, while 75 per cent of schools lack sanitation facilities. Then comes the most ghastly part of the report. 'A serious concern we would like to highlight is that teachers and the school administration force girls and children from the Scheduled Caste [Dalit] communities to clean toilets,' noted the Bharat Bal Vigyan Samiti. 'These children face discrimination because they belong to the Scheduled Caste communities, thereby reinforcing the evil of untouchability and caste roles of traditional societies.'

Clean India remains distant. The Parliamentary Committee on Rural Development (2017-18) report was submitted to the Lok Sabha on 19 July 2018. Headed by Dr. P. Venugopal of the AIADMK, an ally of the BJP, the report noted that 'total sanitation for all and a clean India is still elusive'. The government had said that 84 per cent of rural area had sanitation coverage by 24 May 2018. The report, however, said, 'the committee while examining the subject was of the view that the sanitation coverage figures seemed to be more on *paper* but the actual progress at the ground level is very lethargic'.

At the end of 2017, the UN Special Rapporteur on the human rights to safe drinking water and sanitation – Leo Heller – visited India. He pointed out the flaws in the implementation of the Swachh Bharat Abhiyan, looking in particular at the coercive tactics used by the government and local bodies against ordinary people. The new policy must not be 'human rights free'. Heller noted in particular,

> In taking steps forward in the realization of the right to sanitation, India may involuntarily contribute to violating the fundamental principle of non-discrimination. Particularly given the generations-

old practice of imposing sanitary tasks onto the lower castes, the growth in number of toilets raises concerns that manual scavenging will continue to be practised in a caste-based, discriminatory fashion.

When Heller was in India, reports came out of violence used to force people to use the government toilets. This began to be known as toilet vigilantism after the murder of Zafar Hussein in Pratapgarh (Rajasthan) in June 2017. He was killed as he objected to municipal employees taking pictures of women defecating in public. As Tikender Singh Panwar, of the Communist Party of India (Marxist), put it in 2017,

> This is not to say that toilets are not needed. The problem is with the way toilets are being thrust upon people. This coercion of forcing toilet vigilantism not only makes the lives of women more miserable but also is harassment to such individuals who are not keen to do this exercise of policing. This coercion at the behest of the state is another form of vigilantism akin to cow policing where specific groups are being targeted. It is not easy for people living in cities to manage their waste, but for the time being we can regulate instead of criminalizing open defecation in villages. It must be ensured that no more Zafar Husseins die because of the government's desperation for open defecation-free status.

VII

In 1927, Dr. B.R. Ambedkar led a historic struggle in Mahad (then part of Bombay Province). Thousands of Dalits and supporters burnt the *Manusmriti* in the public programme. They attacked this text for its anti-human sentiments. In the speech at Mahad, Ambedkar compared this gathering to the French

Revolution of the 18th century. Ambedkar, along with scores of his followers, led a Satyagraha at the Chavdar pond by drinking water from it. There act was a rebellion against the dominant caste view that only caste Hindus should drink water from the pond: if a Dalit drinks water, then they pollute all the water.

Ambedkar said that all Dalits should shun professions that stigmatize them, that are seen to be polluting. No Dalit should 'skin the dead animals of the Hindus, shall carry it or eat the carrion', they pledged. In an article after Mahad, Ambedkar wrote, 'The object of these resolutions was twofold. The one object was to foster among the Untouchables self-respect and self-esteem. This was a minor object. The major object was to strike a blow at the Hindu Social order'. The 'water had caught fire', as Dalits remember this *Mahad Kranti*.

Ninety years later, billboards appeared around New Delhi Railway Station that showed Ambedkar – the leader of the *Mahad Kranti* – as an icon of cleanliness. The images showed a man who looked like Ambedkar leading people towards a dustbin to throw garbage. The headline was particularly galling – *Aap ke andar ke Babasaheb ko Aap Jagrut Karein. Gandagi ke khilaf is Mahan Abhiyan mein apna yogdan dein* (Wake up the Spirit of Babasaheb Ambedkar and participate in this Great Campaign of cleaning rubbish).

What does this advertisement suggest? It says that the ruling dispensation – led by the BJP – sees Dr. Ambedkar as nothing more than a person who belongs to an oppressed caste, whose members are supposed to engage in cleaning. This is Dr. Ambedkar, the man who drafted the Constitution, a great scholar with a personal library with more than twenty thousand books, who led a struggle against caste hierarchy and the caste system. But all this seems to mean nothing.

Groups that emerge out of the Ambedkar movement and

others protested these billboards. They were then removed. But who put up these billboards? The erection of the billboards is itself an act of 'human rights free' Clean India. They reinforce the caste system and caste hierarchy. They sanitize oppression.

FIVE. *FASCINATED BY MANU*

I

When the Indian Constitution was promulgated, Dr. Ambedkar said that it had 'ended the rule by Manu'. And yet, Manu seems back, his magnum opus *Manusmriti* in the news on a regular basis. The *Manusmriti*, it needs to be said, was put together between the 2nd century BCE and the 3rd century CE.

In October 2018, three members of the Republican Party of India (Kharat group) – an Ambedkarite organization – marched from Aurangabad (Maharashtra) to Jaipur (Rajasthan). Sheela Bai Pawar, Kanta Ramesh Ahire and Dawood Shakeel Sheikh heard that there was a statue to Manu in front of the Jaipur High Court. This statue had been installed there in 1989, during the government of Bhairon Singh Shekhawat – an RSS leader. Dalit organizations had protested this installation from then onwards. A meeting at the Court in 1989 had decided to remove the statue, but VHP leader Acharya Dharmendra had filed a public interest litigation (PIL) to stop the removal. The High Court stayed the removal, saying that the matter should be taken up by a bench of more than two judges, including the Chief Justice. Nothing further happened. The statue remained, which is why Pawar, Ahire and Sheikh arrived at the Court.

The two women – Pawar and Ahire – climbed onto the statue and blackened the face of the statue. People gathered around and began to attack the women. One man said, '*Main Brahman hoon. Mere pe pot kaalikh* (I am a Brahmin. I dare you to blacken my face).' The women were taken into custody and charged with hurting religious sentiments. They were released on bail.

Their act was seen to hurt religious sentiments. But the defence of Manu is not seen to hurt anyone's sentiments, even as Manu's text is deeply offensive to anyone who believes in equality and liberty.

There is a statue of Ambedkar near the Court. But it is hidden in a corner.

Sambhaji Bhide (age 85), the founder of the Shivpratishthan Sanghatana, gathered his supporters – *Dharkaris* – at JM Road in Pune (Maharashtra) without any police permission. Bhide told his *Dharkaris* to work towards forming a Hindu Nation. The *Manusmriti*, he said, is superior to the teaching of the saints of Dnyaneshwar and Tukaram, that in fact the text of Manu is greater than any other.

> Human beings are animals, but what makes them different is the religion that they follow since animals don't have the idea of religion in them. The capability for self-realization is given by god to the human beings. Being capable to control mind is the way for following a religion. You need to be able to control your mind. Sant Dnyaneshwar and Sant Tukaram told us the way for this. But Manu was a step ahead of these saints. Only religion can save the country.

That Bhide so openly attacked the *sants* of the Bhakti movement raised the question of why he was not arrested for hurting the religious sentiments of people. He was not arrested. He was also not arrested for his alleged role in the Bhima Koregaon violence of January 2018, despite an FIR being framed against him in the heat of the violence. What clouded the headlines was his statement that mangoes from his farm helped infertile couples conceive a child.

This nonsense was the cloud that came between understanding his real role and the dismissal of him. Bhide is seen as the guru of Modi and the mentor of Maharashtra Chief Minister Devendra Fadnavis. Modi often gets summoned by him and comes, 'not on his request but on his order'.

Acharya Dharmendra, Sambhaji Bhide and any follower of Hindutva sees Manu as worthy of respect and love. For them, the *Manusmriti* is more important than the Constitution.

II

Just two weeks before the 90th anniversary celebrations of the Mahad Satyagraha, towards the end of 2017, the leading ideologue of the RSS Indresh Kumar took part in a programme called *Chanakya Gana Samiti* in Jaipur. The theme for the discussion was *Adi Purush Manu ko Pehchanein, Manusmriti ko Janein* (Know Adipurush Manu, Understand *Manusmriti*). The invitation to the event described the *Manusmriti* as 'opposed to caste discrimination and the caste system'. Kumar told the audience that Manu was not only against the caste system, but he was also against inequality. He suggested that historians had presented a confusing picture of Manu. Manu, he said, was the world's first jurist in the field of social harmony and social justice. Kumar's speech came just after Pawar and Ahire had blackened the face on the statue of Manu in front of the High Court.

In 1949, when the Constitution was being formulated, the RSS chief Golwalkar wrote,

> But in our constitution there is no mention of the unique constitutional developments in ancient Bharat. Manu's laws were written long before Lycurgus of Sparta or Solon of Persia. To this day laws as enunciated in the Manusmriti excite the admiration of the

> world and elicit spontaneous obedience and conformity. But to our constitutional pundits that means nothing. (*Organiser*, 30 November 1949.)

Ten years previously, in his *We or Our Nationhood Defined*, Golwalkar had affirmed Manu's hierarchy of humanity.

> The Virat Purusha, the Almighty manifesting himself [according to the *Purusha sukta*], sun and moon are his eyes, the stars and the skies are created from his *nabhi* [navel] and Brahmin is the head, Kshatriya the hands, Vaishya the thighs and Shudra the feet. This means that the people who have this fourfold arrangement, i.e., the Hindu People, is [sic] our God. This supreme vision of Godhead is the very core of our concept of 'nation' and has permeated our thinking and given rise to various unique concepts of our cultural heritage.

In 1942, Golwalkar gave a speech at an RSS camp (this speech is quoted by Jaydev Dole in his *RSS*). The speech is worthy of a long extract:

> One remembers the story of Lord Manu and the fish in this connection. Once, Manu saw a fish outside water which was about to die. He felt pity over it and put it in his pot *(kamandal)*. Within no time the fish started growing and the pot became too small for the fish. Manu transferred it to a pond and slowly when the pond was also found to be too small for the fish, Manu first transferred it to a rivulet then to a river and then to a sea. When there was a huge deluge and the world was about to end the mammoth sized fish saved Lord Manu by carrying him on its feet. When the cataclysm was over – Manu recreated the world. RSS is growing like that fish. The whole world finds itself in cataclysmic situation, people are looking scared

> looking at the present grave situation and are running helter skelter and are trying to save themselves. There is anarchy everywhere. People are so scared that they are ready to embrace a lion but Sangh is telling them with tremendous determination that if Hindu society gets organized then it can save its religion and itself from this storm. An organized society can even save itself from a sky falling with tremendous force. (Translated from Marathi)

Dole notes a few important points about this speech. First, that Golwalkar connects the RSS to the *Manusmriti*. The speech was made on the 15th anniversary of the Mahad Satyagraha, when Ambedkar and his followers had burnt the *Manusmriti*. Golwalkar drew a thick line between the RSS view for India and Ambedkar's view of India. Second, India was in the midst of a major anti-colonial uprising – the Quit India movement – which the RSS had not joined. Without commenting on the mass uprising which terrified the British rulers, Golwalkar tells the Hindus to move to the RSS, an organization with no role in the anti-colonial struggle. He counsels passivity and a glance backwards. K.R. Maḷkani, a leader of the RSS, admits in his book *The RSS Story* that Golwalkar 'saw no reason why Hindu law should break its ancient links with the *Manusmriti*'.

Golwalkar was not alone in his fascination with Manu's book. V.D. Savarkar, who created the doctrine of Hindutva, deeply admired the book and felt it should be the Indian Constitution. In a text on women in the *Manusmriti*, Savarkar wrote,

> *Manusmriti* is that scripture which is most workable after the *Vedas* for our Hindu nation and which from ancient times has become the basis of our culture – customs, thought and practice. This book for centuries has codified the spiritual and divine march of our nation. Even today the rules which are followed by crores of Hindus in their

lives and practice are based on *Manusmriti*. Today *Manusmriti* is Hindu law.

From Savarkar and Golwalkar to the present, there has been a twin move to denigrate the Constitution of India and to uphold the *Manusmriti*, to cast aside the text of equality and substitute it for a text of hierarchy.

III

In 2017, RSS head Mohan Bhagwat addressed the Akhil Bharatiya Adhivakta (Advocates) Parishad in Hyderabad. Bhagwat said that the Constitution was written 'based on foreign sources', which is 'something we must address'. He wanted the Constitution to be changed 'in line with the value systems of the country'. A few months later, Union Minister Ananth Hegde of the BJP said at an event in Karnataka that the Constitution should be changed and 'it will be changed in the days to come'.

Bhagwat and Hegde are not outliers. The election manifestos of the BJP have routinely called for a review of the Indian Constitution. When Atal Bihari Vajpayee of the BJP was the prime minister (1999-2004), he appointed the National Commission to review the working of the Constitution, led by Justice M.N.R. Venkatachaliah. It submitted the final report in 2002, but that could not go anywhere due to the weakness of Vajpayee's government.

When Uma Bharti of the BJP was chief minister of Madhya Pradesh, she pushed an ordinance to ban cow slaughter with an official statement in January 2005 that extolled the virtues of the *Manusmriti*. '*Manusmriti*', the statement reads, 'ranks the slaughterer of cow as predator and prescribes hard punishment for him.' This was the first time in independent India's legal history that an ordinance or a law was based on the *Manusmriti*.

The attempt to discredit the Constitution and to revive the *Manusmriti* is not accidental. It is decidedly part of the RSS-BJP agenda. There is a project to deny human rights to the vast majority of women and to the oppressed castes. Golwalkar did not take kindly to the affirmative action programmes undertaken by the newly independent state for the welfare and empowerment of Dalits and Adivasis. He expressed his disapproval by saying that rulers were digging at the roots of Hindu social cohesion and destroying the spirit of identity that held various sects of Hinduism into a harmonious whole in the past. Denying that the Hindu social system was responsible for the plight of the lower castes, he held constitutional safeguards for them as responsible for creating disharmony:

> Dr. Ambedkar had envisaged the special privileges for 'Scheduled Castes' for only 10 years from the day we became a republic in 1950. But it is going on, being extended. Continued special privileges on the basis of caste only, is bound to create vested interests in them in remaining as a separate entity. That would harm their integration with the rest of the society.

IV

> The laws of Manu relating to the Status of the Shudra make a very interesting reading for the simple reason that they have moulded the psychology of the Hindus and determined their attitude towards the Shudras who form at the present and at all times the most numerous parts of Hindu society. They are set out below under separate heads so that it may be possible for the reader to have a complete idea of the status given by Manu to the Community of Shudras.
>
> – Dr. B.R. Ambedkar

Modi says that he is a 'disciple' of Dr. Ambedkar. A gulf separates them, particularly when it comes to Manu.

Modi is a bhakt of Hindutva. We have already seen that the gurus of Hindutva are champions of Manu's work, something that sets them apart from Dr. Ambedkar. In Modi's book *Jyotipunj* – which first appeared in Gujarati in 2008 – he profiles the lives of 15 RSS workers, most of whom are unknown outside the Sangh. Golwalkar gets the longest treatment. Modi describes him as a good organizer, as a dedicated man and as a man of great intellect. Modi does not disagree with Golwalkar at all, least of all on his views on Manu.

As chief minister of Gujarat and as prime minister of India, Modi has not shown himself to be seized of the crimes of the caste system and of caste hierarchy. This is despite his own stories of being a victim of the asymmetries of the caste system. His rush into a bill to give 10 per cent reservations for dominant castes shows his fealty to these groups. There has been no fundamental challenge to the worldview of the *Manusmriti*.

Modi's views on cleanliness show that he has absorbed the worst of the caste system. Worse yet is his fascination with ancient India. In parliament, Modi said that 'India did not get democracy due to Pandit Nehru', but got it from its 'rich history', the 'many examples of rich democratic traditions that date back centuries. Democracy is integral to this nation and is in our culture'. What might he refer to when he says that democracy is 'in our culture'? In what way could the hierarchies of caste be understood as democratic?

Professor D.N. Jha took to *The Indian Express* to set Modi right on his claims about ancient India, saying that 'knowledge of history has never been a strong point of the RSS from whose ranks Modi has risen to become the prime minister'. On the question of the republican states in ancient India, Jha writes,

> Had he any familiarity with ancient Indian history he would have known that the tribal assembly (santhagara) was dominated by oligarchs and that non-Kshatriyas, slaves and wage earners had no place in it. Members of the assembly bore the title raja or king; in the case of the Licchavis 7,707 rajas, all Kshatriyas, sat in the assembly and the head of their state was a senapati, the term denoting commander in a monarchy. Far from being a democracy, the Licchavi state was an oligarchy.

These states exercised strict control over their subjects through executive edicts and legislation which exposed their undemocratic character, namely how they formulated rules related to the marriage of girls or how they prohibited inter-dining among the people of 'unequal birth'. Then, Jha wrote,

> Rules such as these were no better than those evolved by the Brahmin authors of the Dharmasutras. A closer scrutiny would show that the governments of the Licchavis, Shakyas and Mallas possessed all the paraphernalia of a monarchical state. One would expect that the prime minister of the largest democracy in the world is better informed about the country's past before articulating his effete and obsolete ideas and misleading the people of the country.

Modi's claims about ancient India do not come from ignorance. They come from a need to celebrate the 'republics of Kshatriyas', the rule of the dominant castes as an ideal for 'democracy'. There is disdain here for modern democratic norms, disdain for the views of people such as Dr. Ambedkar.

V

Sangh intellectuals are preparing the ground for two things: first, to absolve the *Manusmriti* for its implication in the violence meted out to Dalits and to women, and second, to divert attention from the caste system and caste hierarchy and point the finger for centuries of violence towards others – mainly Muslims. It is to this end that the Sangh intellectuals seek to produce a 'suitable Ambedkar', an Ambedkar who will help them in this dual diversion.

Books, articles and pamphlets written by Sangh intellectuals routinely tend to glorify the *Manusmriti*, with Ambedkar as part of their arsenal. K.V. Paliwal's *Manusmriti aur Ambedkar* (Hindu Writers Forum, 2007) is one example. Paliwal writes regularly for Suruchi Prakashan, a press close to the RSS, which has published books whose titles betray his point of view, *Isaiyat ki Asaliyat* (The Reality of Christianity), *Jihad Kya aur Kaise?* (What is Jihad and How to Wage It?), *Bharat Islami Rajya ki Or* (India Towards an Islamic State), *Hindu Jagran: Kyon aur Kaise?* (Why Hindu Awakening and How). In the Preface to *Manusmriti aur Ambedkar*, Paliwal writes about the need to revisit the *Manusmriti*. He writes,

> This book has been written for those people who are rather confused about Manu's *Manusmriti* and feel that it supports the present caste system, upper class-lower class and untouchability. The second aim of the book is to remove this confusion that Manu was opposed to Shudras and women and was a supporter of Brahminism. It's third aim is to remove the mistaken understanding spread by modern era social reformer and Dalit leader Dr. Bhimrao Ambedkar. Here all quotes have been excerpted from Babasaheb Dr. Ambedkar *Sampoorna Wangmay*, Volumes 1 to 14 (Appendix 1).

> Dr. Ambedkar has himself admitted that he cannot claim mastery over the Sanskrit language (*Who Were the Shudras*, Volume 13, Page 3). Unfortunately, Dr. Ambedkar wrote on *Manusmriti* basing himself on the anti-Veda scholar Max Müller's edited version, which was rendered into English by George Bühler, which caused many confusions. If instead of Bühler, he would have referred to the version translated by Rangnath Jha and published in 1920-24, then it would have caused less confusions. In his writings on Hindu religion, Dr. Ambedkar has repeatedly used 475 shlokas/stanzas from *Manusmriti* repeatedly. Out of which 200 shlokas are related to women, brahmins and shudras only, most of which are mixed/adulterated. If we remove these mixed/adulterated and anti-Veda Shlokas then we find that no difference remains between Manu and Ambedkar. (Translated from Hindi)

Paliwal's preface further tells us that the around 56 per cent of the shlokas or stanzas in the *Manusmriti* out of the total 2,865 shlokas are later additions. He refers to Dr. Surendra Kumar, who has supposedly revised the *Manusmriti* taking into consideration these so called 'adulterations' and even published a *Vishudh Manusmriti* (Pure *Manusmriti*) in 1985. Paliwal says, 'If this pure *Manusmriti* would have been available in English by 1935 itself then Dr. Ambedkar would have considered differences among *Varnas* as natural and there would have been no opposition to *Manusmriti* then.' Paliwal's book is supposedly meant to remove these 'confusions in a logical way'.

The attempt to sanitize the *Manusmriti* has been a long project of the Sangh intellectuals, even if this sanitization means revision of the 'ancient Hindu scriptures'. In 2017, Amir Chand, a leader of the *Sanskar Bharati*, one of the affiliated organizations of the RSS, urged the Minister of Culture Mahesh Sharma (of the BJP and the RSS) to promote activities so that a 'correct image of the ancient Hindu scriptures' can be presented to the public. Chand was worried that the scriptures appeared to be anti-Dalit and anti-women. These portions had to be whitewashed. New research was needed for this re-branding of the *Manusmriti*.

> Manu was born 8,000 years ago. There are several versions of *Manusmriti*, which have been written 5,500 years after his birth and thus the credentials of the authors and their writings need to be questioned. It is a matter of research, someone needs to look into this.

Amir Chand's proposal has its basis in the journalist Suryakant Bali's *Bharat Gaatha* (Jagriti Prakashan, 2015). This book that the RSS claims is scholarly does not identify its sources to support its claims.

VI

> It was Sir T. Madhava Rao who speaking of Hindu Society of his time said, 'The longer one lives, observes, and thinks, the more deeply does he feel that there is no community on the face of the earth which suffers less from political evils and more from self-inflicted or self-accepted or self-created, and therefore avoidable evils, than the Hindu Community.' This view expresses quite accurately and without exaggeration the necessity of social reform in Hindu Society. The first Social Reformer and the greatest of them all is Gautama Buddha. Any history of Social Reform must begin with him and no history of Social Reform in India will be complete which omits to take account of his great achievements.
>
> – Dr. B.R. Ambedkar, *The Untouchables and Pax Britannica*, 1931

Did Dr. Ambedkar misread the *Manusmriti*, as Paliwal claims? To say so demeans a great intellectual, a man who understood precisely what he was reading and how to read it. His vast writings, his range of topics and his depth of knowledge shows that he was not merely skimming the surface of texts such as *Manusmriti* and those others that allowed Ambedkar to contextualize Manu's work.

In Ambedkar's writings lie an incomplete manuscript – *Revolution and Counter-revolution in Ancient India* – which has been published in Volume 3 of the works of Ambedkar. He had planned to write seven books as part of this enormous project, although he could not finish his work. Ambedkar was going to argue that Buddhism was the most important revolution in ancient India. It was defeated by a counter-revolution led by the Brahmins. In his sketch, Ambedkar had drawn up thirteen chapters, which are as follows:

1. Ancient India on Exhumation
2. The Ancient Regime – The State of the Aryan Society
3. A Sunken Priesthood
4. Reformers and Their Fate
5. The Decline and Fall of Buddhism
6. The Literature of Brahminism
7. Triumph of Brahminism
8. The Morals of the House – *Manusmruti* or the Gospel of Counter-Revolution
9. Philosophic Defence of Counter-Revolution (Krishna and his *Gita*)
10. Analysis of *Virat Parva* and *Uddyog Parva*
11. Brahmins vs. Kshatriyas
12. The Shudras and the Counter-Revolution

13. The Women and the Counter-Revolution

For Ambedkar, *Manusmriti* is a 'record of the greatest social revolution that Hindu Society has undergone'. He understands the text to be a law book – part ethics and part religion. Ambedkar calls the *Manusmriti* the 'gospel of counter-revolution'. The objective of this counter-revolution, Ambedkar noted 'was to destroy Buddhism and re-establish Brahminism'. The text, Ambedkar pointed out, accords special privileges to Brahmins and uses tremendous violence to assert and maintain Brahmin power.

Why was Brahminism opposed to Buddhism? One of the main reasons is that Buddhism hits at the root of Brahminism – it denounces the caste system and caste hierarchy. It might very well be true that the caste system was not as rigid then as it later became, but nonetheless Buddhism attacked the principle of hierarchy. Buddha's views were implemented, so that Buddhism came as a direct assault on the idea of purity and the humiliation of the Shudra. All people would be equal as Bhikkus. This was the essence of the Buddhist attack on Brahminism. For good reason, therefore, the *Manusmriti* castigates the Buddhists as heretics. Three provisions, all quoted by Ambedkar, define the animosity that the *Manusmriti* had for the Buddhists, those whom Ambedkar respected and joined in 1956:

1. Men who abide in heresy . . . the king should banish from his realm (IX. 225).
2. These robbers in disguise, living in the king's realm constantly injure the worthy subject by the performance of their misdeeds (IX. 226).
3. Libations of water shall not be offered to (the souls of) those who (neglect the prescribed rites and may be said to) have been born in vain, to those born in consequence of an illegal mixture

of the castes, to those who are ascetics (of heretical sects) and to those who have committed suicide (V. 89).

VII

In an important unpublished manuscript entitled *Philosophy of Hinduism*, Dr. B.R. Ambedkar draws a straight line from the *Manusmriti* to Friedrich Nietzsche to the Nazis. This text was likely written in the late 1930s or the early 1940s, because Ambedkar writes of Nazism in the present tense, the Nazis not having yet been defeated by 1945. 'The Nazis,' Ambedkar writes, 'trace their ancestry from Nietzsche and regard him as their spiritual parent. Hitler has himself photographed beside a bust of Nietzsche; he takes the manuscripts of the master under his special guardianship; extracts are chosen from Nietzsche's writings and loudly proclaimed at the ceremonies of Nazism as the New German Faith.' It is undisputed, Ambedkar writes, that Nietzsche was beloved by the Nazis.

Meanwhile, Ambedkar writes, Nietzsche's ideas of the Superman – which so appealed to Hitler – came directly from *Manusmriti*. In his *The Anti-Christ* (1888), Nietzsche writes with great feeling of the 'Law Book of Manu'. A few years earlier, Nietzsche's *Thus Spake Zarathustra* (1883) seemed to have the lawgiver Zarathustra modelled on Manu, with Ambedkar claiming that '*Thus Spake Zarathustra* is a new edition of *Manu Smriti*'. For Nietzsche, the Brahmins became the class of Supermen.

Ambedkar quotes from the *Manusmriti* – 'let a Shudra serve a Brahmin' – and then says, 'Hinduism is the gospel of the supermen and it teaches that what is right for the supermen is the only thing which is called morally right and morally good.' These are powerful words. It is hard to parse them out and to say that Ambedkar has neither done his reading or read erroneously. He reads into Nietzsche and sees the implications of Manu's text. And these implications are fascistic. 'The parallel to this philosophy of Hinduism,' he writes, 'is to be found in Nietzsche', which slips neatly a half century after he wrote these texts into the fantasies of Nazism.